The Killer
Detective Novelist

by

mark damon puckett

ONION SCRIBE

PUBLISHING

Onion Scribe Publishing

Cover & Interior Design by Scribe Freelance | www.scribefreelance.com

Cover photograph and manipulation by Bill Havranek

ISBN: 978-0-9835435-2-7

www.markdamonpuckett.com

Published in the United States of America

ALSO BY MARK DAMON PUCKETT

The Reclusives
YOU with The Ill-usives

The character holding the pen has to wrestle and conspire with the one taking shape on paper, extracting a vision of the self from internal darkness—a self dying into fiction as it comes to birth.

—Ross Macdonald,
On Crime Writing

I thank the gods for giving me a brother who was able by his moral character to rouse me to vigilance over myself ...

—Marcus Aurelius,
Meditations

For my man Tim Mehnert,
for the watches—
and the watches over me

CHAPTER ONE
The Relief of Death

He had a weak spot for the dead, some kinship with quiet bodies. It put the silence in him, made him quieter. He felt complicity with death, lauding its terminatory potency, a giant hand slapping down human flies, crushing so many with one swat.

He did not like the dying.

And he did not like the living.

It was with death itself only that he had this affinity, attraction even. He loved death. He desired it. He couldn't wait to die himself.

If death were a person, it would be his nightly drinking friend.

Being alone, that is, loneliness, was a particularly different mortality, a daily repetition of feeling alien on alive sidewalks, a governor of nothing. And sometimes he was such a stranger, so saliently dead-but-walking, that when he finally happened upon another death, finding a dead body, that is, it was as if his recognition of the dead merged with his own dead self, and in some odd negation, he grew comfortable, never repulsed.

Only death brought him back to living.

This body on the floor (how many deaths this week?) was so frail that lumps of bone pressed under her skin.

Mack Harris stared down at her face.

Feminine, he thought, even with the vomit on her neck.

He grimaced and let out a breath, but he still had to run his index finger across the bile and taste it, knowing that he would retch.

You had to touch the dead, he thought. His gagging surged, was suppressed. You had to touch people even when they had died because they probably just had not been touched enough when they were living. This was the essence of all the current irritability steaming from everyone's noses, being untouched, living by neighbors and never inviting them into your house, snarling at faces simply because, deep down, you only wanted to talk to them.

She had fallen from her bed and lay sprawled on her back. A constellation of red, white and yellow pills was dotted on the floor around her bleeding head, reddened blue eyes orbiting in the blood. The red and the white and the yellow were so bright that they glowed, but the red of the pills was different from the red of the blood. Real blood was brown.

Sadness rushed up from in him; it had started as nausea but changed into to something simpler. What began inside never came out as what it had been. The grief, first in his stomach, emerged only as water around his eyes.

How was this?

How did things that were once so strong weaken into other things?

Grief for the dead; it changed itself all the time. Grief was perfect when it started, distorted when it finished. He could only conclude that what trueness of pain originated in a person was perfect, for a second at least, and then it became the wrong version, nothing like it was, a simulacrum of what had originally made it grand.

Inside is grander, he thought. *My outside is not real.*

Rage, a thick needle in a small vein, punctured him because of these contradictions. He had no way of reconciling what was in with what was out and thought of John 20:17 to calm his mind. "Noli me tangere," a resurrected Jesus warns Mary Magdalene. "Keep your hands off me."

Was Christ angry for being alive once more?

To have been dead and forced to live again seemed the worst doom. And was he hungry, having not eaten while he was dead? Did this esurience give Christ a hollow stomach and make him irritable? Was this same hunger the reason he was aggravated with Mary Magdalene?

Mack knew why Christ did not want to be touched, for he was still dead in his own thoughts. To be touched by Mary would mean to acknowledge life. To not be touched would allow him to remain in the posture of death. Christ's limen, therefore, was an impossible threshold, for he was alive but just formerly dead, and the only way he could remain in this nexus was by simply using semi-threatening language to a woman who loved him.

Don't touch me.

One thing was clear: Christ loved death more than life.

Mack held the grand in him like Christ's liminal place. Christ had known actual death. And when he lived again, he had the memory of death. Mack held each death he saw within him, and these memories were not unlike what Christ had done after he had re-lived.

It was a resistance, certainly, this fixation on death as better than life.

What was inside him was not necessarily privacy as most people saw it.

It was also not sacred, which was a terrible, misused word.

It was internal.

Leave the inside of me alone.

There were no perfect words for the internal. How could you create language for what was impossible to define, one's immanence? Definitions were traps, words pretending to articulate ideas but only capturing them in the end. God, *naming* God, was the worst reduction of all.

Follow me, Mack said to himself.

Just follow my head.

I am making sense.

I see *it*, sense.

I see sense.

Why then does nothing come out as what it should be?

The best people were the ones who knew the maze of language.

The novelist!

He had to find the novelist.

He loved the novelist and his writing lightning.

Mack was just like the writer. Only he, Mack, could not express himself.

The writer could.

In his head, yes.

Out of his head, no.

This is why he needed the novelist.

He also knew that the novelist plagiarized his insanity.

Which was fine. Since Mack couldn't do it himself, he was glad someone else could.

The novelist gave him money from the stories he wrote about Mack. There had been at least two books.

Yes, the novelist had stolen from him, in some eyes.

In Mack's (eyes), he had expressed what was only locked in his own head.

The novelist was a vulture who came at the right time. Weren't vultures gorgeous, though, on the side of the road, eating death as if it was a normal dinner?

You had to admire vultures.

Serious birds.

Many would say the novelist was bad for Mack; he (the novelist) was not, however, because he gave Mack what he required. Mack needed for someone to know about what he thought; this was important.

Also, the novelist calmed him because he listened to Mack, just sat there and heard him. When those books were out, Mack read and reveled in them, mostly because the novelist had conveyed it correctly! Had this writer listened so well, or was the old novelist prone to his own legitimate darkness too?

Hmm.

Mack kind of loved the novelist.

The novelist was poor and yet spent all his time around stories. All he cared about were stories. He was terribly unhealthy, eating mostly blue cheese and pretzels and smoking Lucky Strikes or red Pall Malls.

What was the novelist's name?

He couldn't remember.

The novelist would give Mack money and have no food for himself, so Mack would buy food and give it back to him. Why did the novelist do that? He had some kind of creed, stealing Mack's stories but giving him money, even when he (the novelist) had no food.

So they shared many meals, drinks, drugs, even cheese together.

Yes, the novelist was all right.

He *tried*. Tried to remain aware while also being an outsider.

Most people he found to be petty and idiotic. Traffic made Mack apoplectic. Dumb cops with double chins pained him. Stupidity of women in pink on cell phones incensed him. Porcine men in suits were the worst. Loud children with no manners disgusted him.

To bring him back to himself, he tapped his chin with his knuckle, Morse code, dit, dat, dat.

He hated himself for hating average people.

In the end everyone was average. Humans were neither failures, nor were they superlative. Mack gave them a C- average.

Right now he absolutely had to figure out what had happened to the dead young girl on the floor. According to her computer, she had been in and out of anorexia centers, denied many times because of insurance. Her laptop was on the bed, and there were several coterminous instant message conversations going. She was also writing multiple letters about her affliction.

Mack read what he needed then printed quickly. He shut the windows and erased her unsent suicide threats to friends, pocketing the copies of the notes.

But he remained.

This was the most difficult aspect of being near the dead. There was a sour cologne that rose from them, right after they had died. It was acrid bliss, smelling a rose inside sickness.

He shouldn't be hovering over the dead.

He had to have a conversation with himself about God now. If he didn't have it about (not with), he would turn so paranoid that he couldn't move, like those schizophrenics whose bodies stiffen into catalepsy, limbs hardening a person into a human statue.

His conversation was a monologue, he admitted. There was no dialogue. Maybe there was dialogue. Or was it just two monologues, falsely stichomythic?

It was like this: Mack was fatigued with praying. To what? Himself. Oh man, the pretending. How did everyone continue pretending so much? What led to these proclivities to falsify comfort in religious fiction? How could he unlearn to pray?

The dead girl, Mack. The dead girl.

He couldn't look down at her now.

He should be thinking like a murderer. He wasn't. He was thinking like a man who obsesses with death.

Crippling.

How had he even ended up in this room? Was his nose for the moribund that atavistic and acute?

Keep your hands off me.

And just do not touch me.

CHAPTER TWO
More About Death

Hours later, he was still standing over the body. He liked being the first one with new death. It was quiet. Still, he hated himself for his endless contempt (for everyone), so he was not without compunction either, beating himself up for talking and cursing under his breath.

Why did he hate the living so much?

He himself was alive.

He loved death no less than a disturbed lover. How could he admire something so awful and gorgeous in its brutality when he could not stand anyone still breathing?

Life had a brutal gorgeousness of its own, yet it was ersatz. Death was never fake; life always was.

Death was an entity more alive than people.

Death was his side world, his soi-disant paracosm.

Death talked to him in the form of some phony mate, walking beside him, annoying him, and yet Mack listened to the voice, saw the companion.

Another part of him knew that death was not real, in life. The pseudo-friend would just show up beside him, asking him questions.

Mack was conscious that his mind was not right (never had been). His head was so messy yet empty, in perpetual anti-social desuetude.

He needed two heads.

However, lately, death was lively. Its personality emerged from air and heckled him with eerie prattle. And when Mack analyzed his "visions" or delusions, he could not figure out why he had been chosen. For that is what he felt, never *I am losing my mind* but *I think, a little bit, that I have been chosen to see this, that I may, perhaps, be the only one who does.*

Stop thinking, Mack.

It *wasn't* thinking though!

It was disuse.

There was no thinking about normalcy.

The social part of his mind had vanished.

Desuetude.

He had simply stopped trying to think of normal things.

And, yes, yes, he thought of death, which meant he was technically thinking of something, but to him, his mind now equated to disuse.

It was not possible to speak to others at times. He merely gazed at them, words thumping in his stomach, never rising higher. If one caught in his throat, it was as if small hands were about to sneak up behind the back of his mouth and asphyxiate the word away. Countless words, thus, never left his gut where they were self-contained, popping around like flecks of sizzling grease.

He was thankful for his detective work, gloomy and atrocious as it was.

He was made for it.

He still could not leave the room.

He had been standing over the body for hours, hours he could not even quantify.

CHAPTER THREE
The Novelist Interrupts

The penuric novelist wants to stop here and give the reader a break from Mack's obsession with death, articulate as it may be (with many thanks to Mack for his mental gratitude toward me).

In truth, the novelist, herein, wants you to think about death as much as possible, and yet one must also not stare too hypnotically at it.

Mack is my surrogate; he takes the psychological heat.

I get to sit back and be heroically lucid to the reader.

Poor Mack.

I put him through so much.

The novelist knows Mack Harris personally, so in effect this is not a true novel, but more of an internalized biography, as imagined through Mack.

There is not one soupçon of fiction in this book. Keep repeating this heuristic epigraph to yourself.

It is important to know that Mack is not a character but an actual person. The novelist became fascinated with him, having lived right across the hallway for many years.

I still live across from Mack.

There is scrutiny, yes; there is obscurity, yes; and there are two people trying to tell a story.

It's never good when two people tell you something.

Maybe it helps to know that the novelist drinks often with Mack, and Mack believes the novelist is death personified, the only true friend who speaks and writes of death as Mack does. Even though this book is absolutely true, it may seem that some quasi-fictive moments give it the illusive sense of being fabricated. Not the case.

Fiction is true.

Well, *good* fiction is insuperable.

I write a different kind of fiction, however (one that has no fiction in it).

Simply put: there is an extravagant creature, truth, and I do my best to honor it; however, since truth contains all falseness, I only do my job by comprehending the microscopic.

To put it a different way, there is, say, a dog. We'll call her a Black Labrador. Her name is Sarah. On Sarah there are white lice. Now, most of the time, Sarah's pink tongue flaps out of her mouth happily, and no one can see the lice. A lice is a nit. I look at the nits, making me a nitpicker. Those nits are the microscopic; moreover, they are tinier truths only novelists take the time to see. And sure, sure, make a joke about how I spend my time focusing on the lice of truth.

I don't care.

I love lice.

Lice *are* truth.

What Mack doesn't realize is that the novelist merely writes of death, whereas Mack has imaginary death friends to whom he speaks while walking.

Some corrections. First) the novelist has done most of the things Mack has addressed, but the novelist has only written one book about him; second) the novelist does give Mack money and Mack gives it back but usually three dollars for a candy bar. Mack doesn't feed the novelist. The novelist has food.

The myths we have about one another, sigh. Even those so close. We mythologize those closest, I think.

At one point, the novelist believes that he has been confused with one of Mack's death friends. Hence, Mack knocks on the novelist's door at three a.m. to palaver about death while trying also to drink away these thoughts.

Mack seems to think that death is alive; this is what fascinates the novelist.

What the novelist and Mack have learned is that these thoughts are embodied in them, that they will never vanish, and that they, Mack and the novelist, will still insist they are temporary, all the while drinking nocturnally, conversing out their demons.

Demons, however, like their drinking friends too much.

New demons are created from the drinking.

Quondam demons appear when there is too much drink.

New and old demons chicken fight while other demons spectate and place bets.

We are not writing a book about demons, no, but about conversations that lead to thoughts, thoughts that lead to narratives, narratives that lead to no conclusion except that it is superfluous to make up narratives.

Fictionless fiction.

Narratives are important.

Narrations are not.

It might be supposed that the novelist is crazier than Mack. After all, I sometimes refer to myself as "the novelist", which stinks of the supercilious. I'm just trying to keep it official. Back in college, I was always told that the third person was "official" and that the first person was "unofficial". I was told this by men with white beards who feared the first person. They were right on some levels.

Sometimes, we just need distance from the first person. Sometimes, on the other hand, we *crave* the first person.

I write of Mack in the third person and even write of myself in the third, but, on occasion, I will invoke first-person-ness.

It's possible, very possible, that I am insaner than Mack.

But we are not in a place to judge either of us.

Have you ever been a novelist, alone in rooms, drunk most of the time, trying to make sense of things (that no one can)?

I.

Or have you been a schizophrenic whose layers of worlds are colored by confusion?

Mack, who thinks he's a detective from black-and-white movies.

If you have been neither of us, it's all right.

This is not a judgmental book.

We are all both novelist and schizophrenic; it is our extremes of these two that we absolutely need to know.

The spectrum, Mack would say.

The unspectrum, the novelist would pseudo-echo.

It's a complicated book.

You have to stick with it.

You do not know how to stop reading this darkly engaging obsessive piece of writing.

You understand without getting it all.

You are doing so well.

A photograph of words.

Some twisting vines of languet, our unstoppable tongues.

Human tempos are elusive, our meters miscellaneous, logaoedic. Some controlling poets would like you to think we are iambic; we are not. Read a dialect atlas sometime, poets!

The dialect of insanity is not in this book.

So lip-lock with the jazz and bounce around with us.

There *will* be jazz a little later.

CHAPTER FOUR
Skirmishing (with Ghosts)

Luckily, the cases kept Mack occupied.

He had his job. Without a case, he turned derelict, sitting in coffee shops and snarling at:

—that woman sweeping too close to him.

—that clueless man in a suit walking too proudly for no reason.

— (and please G(g)od stop the cell phones)

Later he would look for a fight on the subway because someone bumped into his body.

Ghost fights.

How much of his life was this mental fighting with people who were always worse in his head than when they were real? Correction: they were pretty bad in person, yes, but much worse in memory.

Mack had slept in the streets and wandered for days at a time with no money to eat. He knew that his moods were worsened by these losses.

Focus.

How did he get here first to this dead girl?

He didn't really know. He was losing his ability to know himself. They said that began to happen to your mind after forty when you had no friends and talked to yourself all the time.

Being hungry didn't help either. Why did he give the novelist his last candy bar!!!

Drinking on an empty stomach sent you down the mental corkscrew.

He talked to the dead. Was it a conversation if one person could not speak?

What did you do to die? he would ask. That was always his first question.

What are you *doing* dead?

People died for four reasons: murder, suicide, accidents, disease. Mack tended to believe that suicides were murder, self-murder yes, but also accompanied by reasons that drove them there.

Other people killed you in some form, in some way. People killed you even when you killed yourself. There was just a secret paper trail for suicide. You had to find out who else had pushed the self-murderer to make it bad enough to die. Either it was a mental or physical disease that caused folks pull the trigger, but it was *people* who pushed them to that point.

He often stared at the dead for a long time, waiting to see what they would tell him.

He had heard about this anorectic girl lying in her pills.

A dead girl.

How long had he been here?

She was famous but not for the usual jejune reasons. She had published a book, graduated from NYU and was a seer of types, maybe a real pagan witch even, reading cards for stars who hired her. She absorbed all the facile lunacy of stardom.

Now what had happened to her?

Dead while chatting on Facebook.

Mack sighed. He squatted to his sore knees that popped like gravel spraying the underside of a car. He touched a jutting bone. There was a richer odor now, not quite rancid, not pleasant either, like smelling sweetness in your own defecation and not wanting to admit you liked it.

He had to go.

He wouldn't wait for police; they hated him; he hated them.

They wouldn't even know he had been here.

He would walk around the room.

He would go to the door and put his hand gently on the knob.

He might even turn the knob.

He wouldn't pull the door.

He would walk back over to the body and think of Michelangelo sneaking into the morgue at night to cut open bodies, to hold up organs and feel them, to understand sinews for his sculptures.

Why did you die? he whispered.

He didn't know how long he stayed.

Thinking of the cadaver dogs used to scent out dead bodies for the police, Mack wondered what those animals thought of death as its smell came into their noses.

He had to find the novelist.

Just some beers with that insane writer had the potential to assuage his intellectual panic.

Before he extricated himself from this magnetized lethargy, this toxically exquisite room, he leaned over and gazed at her mouth. Her top lip trickled blood, barely perceptible dots, like tiny red ants.

"Hmm," he muttered.

CHAPTER FIVE
Noises

Outside, his mind was cluttered with a sudden thought of a silent library with one man typing too loudly, aggressively, the typing drilling in his head, a jack-hammerer on a typewriter. He was so attuned to these head noises that they disturbed him every few seconds.

He was obsessed with all the ways people tried to kill you, down to the smallest thing.

Walking down the street, he could often be seen stopping suddenly and shaking his head from side to side, a dog flicking off annoying rain water.

Besides the novelist, whom could he see next?

Ah, he already knew the little person he needed to see.

But he wouldn't go straight there.

Crunch!

The little crunch man held the truth, he felt.

Mack would find him.

Mack could say he was lost.

He was not.

He liked to lose what others could not handle losing.

Others.

A battle.

Sometimes "others" got too close.

His head, though smeared with regurgitated Kandinsky colors, was clear.

Others.

What separates Mack from the novelist is so simple.

Mack is inside, inside his head.

The novelist is empty, has no head but for others. Others are his head. His interviews with Mack necessarily define him.

Mack sees this so well, finally.

He has always been trying to figure out the novelist.

Nothing exists outside of Mack's head.

Nothing exists inside the novelist's writing.

To clarify: the novelist absolutely needs Mack deeply.

To clarify: Mack needs the novelist deeply.

First to beers with the novelist.

Then to the little crunch man.

And at some point, to Chloe.

He could not be responsible for knowing the order of these things.

Lineally, like a prince almost a king, this narrative has a filial contour in the anarchy.

Contours are so often perceived as curves, yet they are lines in the end.

Our story is a contoured narrative.

CHAPTER SIX
Chloe?

It was tough being loathed. Still, it gave you an insular privacy. He walked up Union Square past Coffee Shop and went straight toward his French girlfriend's pied-à-terre, staring at the building, a crossword puzzle of tenancy, each window a box, each person a letter.

Chloe was an eye model (the left eye; it was insured) and smoked thin cigars. She was upset about her accent and how it held her back from getting roles in "real" films. Hence, she was painful to be around these days, her ego bordering on ludicrous. It was as if she were in a bad French film with an average American plot. (In Mack's defense, this last sentence was the novelist's.)

Wait, what did that actually mean?

He shook his head from side to side.

He dreaded being around her these days. She would come home from auditions with this hostile scowl, the face of a rejected person, a mask of surliness and silent irascibility.

In truth he dreaded being around everyone.

This was the consequence of a crowded world: you were forced up close with all the people you previously despised at a distance.

Loud headphones.

Cruel glances.

He couldn't stand music when it was forced on him!

And intimacy with another only led to holding in your gas, the fumes of yourself internalizing, combusting in your intestines as you pretended. You pretended to love in this manner, crippling your gut in the process.

Why did we do it?

Why did we fake our way through lives?

Suddenly, Mack realized that "the classroom" was an anagram for "schoolmaster". Whew, he thought, feeling better for finally seeing this.

Order hid itself in anagrams, implying a necessary rearranging to find the clandestine new word. The letters were there; you merely had to move them.

You could reorder things and find another type of order.

Only the very front seats in cinemas gave him any solace. It was the best comparison to death that he could find: sitting in the front row with a large screen of images, neck craned, avoiding the noisy people.

He heard many voices all the time, never able to isolate one, a mumbling choir of bees that sounded like they were discussing him, even singing about their plans to sting him.

At least he was conscious of how he was, knowing that he made situations worse.

Which is why he stayed to himself mostly.

Or went to films.

He figured out most of his cases through films.

He listened to the detectives of the past.

Another reason for others to judge him. "You watch films to solve your cases?!"

Yes, he did. He knew that the past noir was the only true mythology of its day. He was convinced of this.

Noir scared you if you were not ready for it.

He was glad for life because noir was in it. And you couldn't have noir in books. It was not the same.

Only film could be noir.

Noir was the dark in your sight. It was that dark that you saw (but acted like you couldn't see).

Ah, noir.

We have Mack and the novelist in absolute violent agreement on this point.

Noir, black, night in French, was not black. Certainly, in an anagrammatic way (iron), it was the only light that had been allowed to be light.

Funny how noir forgets its own radiance.

Look at noir.

Look closely at it.

It is also anagrammatically iron.

Monochromatic.

Dark, light.

Both.

And yet noir wins.

Calling it lumière would sound silly.

Because these are films that have more light than black.

Why, then, does dark win?

Because dark, finally, is noir.

Dark is iron.

Being around people would always lead to some inscrutable conflict that baffled Mack.

So he would do justice to the dead bodies and find the details all the other mediocre klutzes would miss.

But he was never unhappy.

He had done very few jobs that actually paid, realizing that most of his pro bono work was just to keep himself out of his head (just like writing, which, also, rarely paid).

Anything to stay out of his head as ideas screwed into his temples to lobotomize him.

When would it get better?

Would it?

Or would he be cursed to see all things, all his life, and only to be comforted by death?

He stared up at Chloe's crossword building and then changed his mind, instead walking back to 14th and over to 2nd Avenue where he drank in a bar for a few hours by himself, waiting for the novelist.

Cheap bourbon shot.

Warm tap beer.

Bourbon shot.

His body warmed with the boozed.

At the other end of the bar was his novelist neighbor, who waved and sent him over a free drink, the bartender placing a shot glass upside-down in front of him.

Mack waved back to the novelist.

How long had he been sitting over there?

Mack didn't mind the novelist. Normally, he would go over and drink with him right away, but they understood each other, that just because you were in the same bar didn't mean you *had* to talk. He would drink with the novelist in a few minutes, but he needed time to think about the blood trickle on the dead girl's lip.

The novelist had helped Mack through difficult visions that had given him raw nightmares. Often, when he awoke from one of them (relieved they were not real), he left his apartment, crossed the hall and knocked. And even if it was late into the night, the novelist always answered.

Yes, the novelist was all right.

Some suits on two bar stools eyed him, a little afraid to be snide because of Mack's size but mocking him just the same. Mack wanted to choke them. He fantasized about the killing. There was nothing he hated more than a suit, the clothing and the metonym. He ordered the free novelist's shot and raised it to him, as the writer raised his own glass to him in a distant toast.

Mack decided to walk over at this point.

They shook hands and sat together on two stools at the bar, not speaking for a moment.

"Well," Mack began, as the bartender quickly poured a couple more of pints of lager for them. "I found another body today."

"Oh yeah?" the novelist replied, sipping the yellowish beer, white suds forming on his top lip.

Mack focused on the white suds mustache.

"Why are you staring at my mouth?"

"Um, she was bleeding, just slightly, from her lip. Your beer reminded me of it. The suds from your beer on your top lip."

The novelist wiped his mouth with the back of his hirsute hand. It looked like an ape's. Man, his hand was hairy. What was the point of hand hair?

"I spent all day with her body."

"Doing what?"

"I don't know, novelist. I couldn't leave. I found it impossible to leave."

Why did the novelist always happen to have a notebook with him? He jotted a few scribbles.

"What are you writing?"

"Just some squibs you tell me, Mack. You're like my own personal newsfeed."

"A new book, perhaps?"

"Perhaps."

Mack sipped his lager; it was now half-full. It was cold and tasted good.

"Is the book also about me?"

"Yes, it is. My writing is always about you."

"Should I tell you about the little crunch man?"

"Who's the little crunch man, Mack?"

"Ah, I will let you know and you can use him. He is quite the character! I can't believe I've never told you about him."

"Do tell," said the novelist, poising his pen nib against the paper, waiting.

"In a bit. First, I want to talk about this dead girl."

"Okay, let's start with her. Whatever order you want."

This was another good thing about the novelist: he allowed Mack to speak in circles, distorted and misshaped circles.

Ovoids.

CHAPTER SEVEN
Surprising

Inebriatedly staggering at Chloe's door, deciding to stay this time, he slid the wobbling key inside the lock.

It was about as easy as locating her seemingly itinerant clitoris, one that tasted of chocolate croissant and coffee when his lips could snare it.

In his absorbed concentration his tongue stuck out the side of his mouth like a pig's nipple.

Before he could even click the key to the right, though, thick knuckles thumped his right cheekbone, sending his drunkard's body dropping to the hallway carpet.

Blind man's light flashed this aching whiteness as if someone had photographed him with a fist.

Then the other person was gone.

Mack was pained to even open his eyes and kept them closed.

Where had the punch come from?

He was so drunk he hadn't seen anyone.

He was certain that he and the novelist had drunk twenty beers each, plus shots.

The suits he had wanted to kill had ended up being fans of the novelist.

When they discovered that Mack was the actual detective-inspiration in his books, well, it had devolved to masculine alcoholism.

[Novelist: Mack thinks often of the novelist in this narrative, giving the impression that the writer is ubiquitously public. He is not. In fact, not many have read the novelist's books. And so it was a surprise that two suits had read me/him. Also, I wrote *one* book about Mack, remember? He keeps thinking there are more. We did get very drunk though, and, yes, the suits, a gay couple, had read my novel. Sorry to interrupt. When Mack is under head trauma, his mind tends to contort storylines more than he already does.]

For a second Mack thought he had lost his balance, maybe passed out, but it was a fist.

He knew a fist.

His poor face sure knew knuckles.

When would people stop hitting him?

He was sort of relieved when these fists finally connected.

They momentarily calmed all the pained anticipation that had filled his days.

This current fist meant that he was *very* close to finding out something about the dead girl.

He couldn't get out any more thoughts, like meat squeezing through a grinder then stopped by a bone.

Thoughts stopped.

CHAPTER EIGHT
Waking

In a film noir he would wake up and know the culprit of the punch.

The owner of the fist would be standing over him with a cigarette in a smart white suit.

It was Mack Harris' opinion that detective stories had started going downhill when everybody stopped wearing good suits.

And hats.

What had happened to those hats?

Men had once tipped their hats to other men.

There was this old film called *Dark Corner* with Lucille Ball, and the mystery hinged on ink spilled on a suit, finding it at one of the many dry cleaners in the city.

There were no simple mysteries like this one anymore.

No one stood over him.

Instead, he just woke by himself with a sore face, still in the hallway, reeking of beer as he smelled his underarms.

"Wow," he said, cringing after a sniff, "that smells like onions and gasoline."

But he couldn't resist the urge to sniff again.

The key remained in the lock, unturned.

Take two.

When he stumbled inside, there were no coffee beans.

The fridge was as cavernous as his stomach.

Hunger kept his mind off his mind.

He liked hunger.

Christ had to have been hungry after being dead for three days.

Plus he didn't really care who had hit him, although he wondered if it related to his inquiring proximity to the dead girl.

Debt collector?

Chloe's ex?

Most likely somebody telling him not to sniff around the dead girl from earlier.

Usually, he got punched about once a week.

He was inured to the fists.

Little did they know that the punches, like hunger, also took his mind off his head.

He was not in a film noir, though, even if he watched too many of them by himself.

He wanted to be in black and white.

That scene in *Blast of Silence* where he falls face first in the water.

You think he will get away, but it is noir after all and simply ends with his death.

Drown, credits.

Same with the pensive hired killer in *Murder by Contract*.

Shot, dead in a tunnel, credits.

Massaging his chin with his fingers, he stared into his vacant open fridge and sighed.

Then he lay on the sofa and slept again, his cat jumping up on his chest, circling and curling into a ball, half-closed sideways almond eyes.

Its warm little body rose and fell with his breaths.

When he awoke, again, Chloe was there this time staring at him with worried annoyance.

The eye model.

He liked to call her the I model.

Models, good lord, they were blank people, deficient, physically brilliant, anti-dimensional.

It was easier *not* to look at them.

"Mackie, I can't do dis anymore."

"Do what?"

"Dis. You coming home whenever you want. I saw you outside yesterday staring at the building. Why did you leave?"

"I'm sorry."

"It makes me miserable."

"You've been miserable for a decade," he reminded her, yawning. Oddly, the cat yawned at the exact same time.

Animals often mimicked him; he would have to look closer at them.

"No worse than yourself," she respewed.

"Leave me alone," he mumbled. "I just got blindsided. Took a nice thump in the hallway."

"It wasn't Oscar again, was it?"

"I don't care who it was."

Who was Oscar? Was that the ex? He always forgot his name.

"You have dat look again."

She sized him up.

"What look?" he replied.

"When you are focused on something besides me."

"Yeah, that's true. I found another dead girl."

Casually, she reached for her packet and knocked out a thin cigar.

She toyed with it before laying it on her bottom lip.

Her lighter rose and the end was fired.

She inhaled and blew the smoke straight up.

Mack watched it float to the light and wondered how killing smoke had so much life.

"Chloe," he almost began and held her name in him. The air from his lungs was there; the word from his brain was there; the mouth's ability to say it was not there.

She saw this.

They were quitting on each other.

Only habit brought them together once in awhile.

There was nothing to tell her anymore and yet he needed her by his side.

He didn't know the reason.

He just wanted her there.

He also wanted her not there.

. . .

The next morning she left his bed without a word, smoke behind her like a wedding gown tail of some walking dead bride.

He sat up and his cat, Arm, appeared from nowhere.

Arm was the only thing he had owned for fifteen years.

Her wide green eyes stared up at him and he knew that he had no food for her.

Stepping onto the wood floor with bare feet, he waited for the hips to crack before moving toward the kitchen.

Chloe had brought him some things, for him and Arm.

Not much, just a few bags on the counter.

Aw.

Coffee beans, cat food, sesame bagels, lox, cream cheese.

He hated being old and unable to afford food for himself or his pet.

There were so many things in life that just became out of your control.

He had given up caring, yet somehow the food always came at the right times.

He had a few friends thinking about him.

Or did, at one time.

Now that he was disappearing into himself, even they had even stopped trying.

He was glad that they had wanted to help, although their guilty bags of rice were more for them than for him.

No one wants to believe that a friend is hungry; it makes sipping the ten-dollar martini (with a two-dollar tip) seem wrong.

He had ceded life; he was somnambulating, half-living but hyper-conscious of the deliquescence.

One emotion plagued him, an ennui that had eaten away the highs and lows, leaving only a steady angst that hovered in the middle, a wire act with no pole to balance him and no net below him.

He was sure that if he fell off the wire, he would kill a couple of clowns practicing below.

Ha, he chuckled out loud, crushed clowns.

When he was hungry, his thoughts were better.

He decided to ignore the food she had brought him (but to feed Arm).

After Chloe left, it was ten a.m., the worst time of the day, all that day ahead and no life to fill it, only thinking about the dead and being less than alive himself.

The dead girl.

If he could only focus on the dead girl!

Why hadn't he done something?

How had he even gotten to her?

And the fist on his face?

Hm.

His reactions were delayed because his body ignored pain at first.

Once it absorbed into him, he was forced to put it on an errand list along with the laundry: "Tasks: 1) Figure out Fist."

He found his jacket and pulled out the printed copies of the dead girl's conversations.

The pages were blank, just white paper.

Turning them over a few times, he wondered how the writing had disappeared.

He noticed his laundry in a pile in the corner, not even in the hamper.

He needed some coffee; the coffee helped him focus.

His cheekbone around the eye stung from the punch.

And his chin had hit the floor first.

He moved his jaw from side to side and more pain ensued.

Who had hit him?

Where had the words gone?

He tried to think, one thought darting to the next like a player caught in a steal between bases, not knowing which direction is best, just doomed to be out.

Now, this would be an ordinary fear for most, a dream perhaps, a man stuck between bases, frozen.

With Mack, though, he stayed frozen, cataleptic (his worst paranoia), and the analogue changed.

Sure, baseball was not much of a threat; it was a game, to be sure.

But here is what would happen with Mack's mind.

The shortstop and third baseman would toss back and forth while Mack ran between them.

This part of the daydream, or whatever it was, was decently amusing until Mack froze.

A hand then picked his frozen body off the field and moved it to a chess board.

Maybe he was a rook.

It didn't matter.

But he could no longer think of baseball, only chess.

After a while, the chessboard would superimpose itself over the baseball field, a layer above it.

And Mack, as a rook, could see himself still frozen on the baseball diamond, exactly in the place he was when the hand had lifted him.

Another hand would intervene at this point, picking up the rook and holding it in mid-air, contemplating a next move.

So there he would be, a rook held in frozen fingers watching himself as a stationary baseball player.

Just like with the dead girl, he could not extricate himself from these two places.

He was life.

She was death.

When there were two things, Mack Harris was flummoxed.

He was an alive man trying to figure out the dead.

He was a rook staring at a former self, an absurd hitter stuck between bases.

To make sense of it, he positioned the chess board hovering over the baseball field into the shape of the diamond.

Diamonds were rotated squares in the end.

Soon, the baseball field looked like a chess board, the pitcher a king, the center fielder a queen.

No, diamonds were *not* squares; they turned on a point, and that point differentiated them.

Mack's mind diverted into strange things he remembered from somewhere.

You could hear corn grow, if you listened.

Seagulls recognized each other by their eye color.

How?!

There were so many seagulls.

So few diamonds.

Normal people would not mix squares and baseball diamonds and corn and seagulls together.

He was compos mentis enough to know this, but something separated him from the ability to disassociate from mental multiplicity.

It was an echopractic representation of chaos, wasn't it?

He mimicked whatever moved into his vision.

Was he *that* quick, aping life as he saw it, some sort of caprine miscreant, eyes hopping psychologically along like a drunk goat?

When was it that he fell in love with language so much, and when did that same language begin to save him in his worst moments?

And as it saved him, why did this language also turn into terra nullius.

Was language a no man's land when it was spoken inward?

Mack would come home from a dead body and open an old red dictionary and run his finger down the words, the finger moving rapidly.

He would take a word and find words within that word.

On a separate piece of white typing paper, he would have to find as many words as possible.

Yes words alleviated other thoughts.

If you crammed new words in you, then other obsessions could not remain.

That was his theory.

On this point, he and the novelist were the same.

Most people were indifferent to language.

They saw it as sort of buying gas, just another part of you that required no reflection.

Not the novelist though.

Whenever Mack was in linguistic doubt, he walked across the hall and was revived in words that relieved him.

The novelist was his language brother.

CHAPTER NINE
A Talk About Writing

On the street he bought black coffee in a blue paper cup from Dmhed, who actually pronounced his name Dumb Head. Mack liked saying, "Thanks Dumb Head," and it being okay. This gave him a smile because Dmhed seemed not to know about the sound of his name, plus the coffee was scalding slick motor oil.

"And how are you, Mr. Mack Harris? How is your new novel coming?"

Coffee cup was handed to him. Steam rose off the black like warm rain on hot asphalt.

"**My** new novel?"

"Yes, last you were here, you spoke of a book you were writing? You said you were 'method-writing', growing your beard, not showering. You told me the title was *The Killer Detective Novelist*. You said it was a book that was causing you much introspection."

"But...I'm not a writer, Dumb Head. Don't you mean my neighbor? He's a novelist. Maybe you mean him?"

"No, ha ha, you have told me you were a writer many times. You even showed me the other book you wrote."

"Ha, oh, no, that was *about* me. The novelist wrote that."

"The novelist?"

"Yes," Mack had to inform him, "my neighbor."

"Mack, I thought you lived in the shelter. Part of your method, right?"

"I am on the streets now. I lost my house. I *was* in the shelter."

"You are famous around here, sir! *Mack Harris Is Morbid* has become a book many of my friends read. You have always been so humble about your book, sir. We are friends, aren't we now? You no longer have to pretend with your humility."

Dumb Head lifted up a book into the window of his coffee truck. Sure enough, it was a book with Mack's name as author.

"Will you sign it? I have always been afraid to ask."

"Do you have pencil?" Mack requested. "I hate signing in pen."

Mack signed the book.

With a yellow pencil.

"And isn't there a film noir coming out, you know, based on the book? Some Russian director?"

"Um, yes?"

He would absolutely need to speak with the novelist.

"I cannot wait for the film. A film at The QUAD! What a dream to have a film of your book showing in this fantastic city. I know you have integrity in your literacy, and I am sure that will translate well into the visual of film."

The man who sold him coffee seemed to know more about him than he did. In point of fact, he was a rather avid reader to be working inside such a small truck all day.

Luckily, when Mack forgot himself, the people who saw him regularly gave him clues, hints that took him back to the quotidian.

Whew.

He could fake himself through most things.

He was lost but also seeing it.

Not that there was an actual novelist, but maybe Mack would need to doppelgangerly invent one to balance him.

He would think about this.

The job ahead was not an easy one.

Side-to-side head shake.

And if he lived in a shelter, why was he in bed with Chloe? Oh yes, that was her place, not his.

He had definitely slept in the shelter a lot lately.

Come to think of it, he was homeless.

Well, anyway, he couldn't think about it anymore.

Had he been drinking with the dead girl? Had she invited him to her room? Had he hurt her?

He needed to talk to a famous friend of the dead girl.

The famous.

Blech.

He had known immediately the person to find first, but he was avoiding him, one, because this person was tedious and, two, because he was famous.

Wait. This famous person was also kind of nice. He liked him. In fact, this famous person was on his side, if not a bit repetitive.

At the buzzer he punched an archaic red square button and heard a voice. There was a pause after he said who he was, then the buzzer clicked open the door.

But there was another door with another buzzer.

This time, he simply buzzed and the door was buzzed open. There would only be a door ajar across from the elevator, for this person never came to greet anyone.

You entered the door and walked to his desk and chair, the sole furniture in the apartment.

This was the playwright's "office".

There were no books or files.

Just a desk with a typewriter and stacks of paper.

Unlike his novelist neighbor, this particular writer was a queerish one.

"Senator! Enter, please."

Mack stared at him. How would you describe such a troglodytic anti-social homunculus? Maybe troglodytic anti-social homunculus would do the trick, but perhaps not. Let's say Truman Capote had entered the machine in *The Fly* and the teleporting had failed. Truman Capote + a fly, thought Mack. This man was small, his eyes like green olives, his pupils red pimentos.

Normally, people with bug eyes also had big heads.

Not this man.

His head was small.

His shoulders narrow.

His chest sunken.

He slouched over his typewriter and continued to peck with two forefingers even as he spoke to Mack without ever looking at him.

He was also dressed like a nun.

"I know a little why you're here," he said.

Mack surmised that silence worked best with the verbose; eventually, they could not help their sesquipedalian propensity to indulge their vocabulary. They would act as if it were the most natural thing in the world to use such words, and yet it was just the deeper insecurity of the brilliant calling attention to itself. He had always liked this writer in front of him who seemed to create plays from another time—about Americans who were more exotic simply because they spoke with different cadences and had less to concern them.

In fact, Mack had seen this man's plays many times, theater that had, at one point, made him want to write also. The feeling passed. Mack tried to write a few one-acts in the same vein, realizing by the end that he was merely copying the man in front of him.

Ah, so maybe Mack was a writer?

Or, at the very least, he had at one point written.

He waited.

Clicks of keys—pressed by fingers of some mad organist—echoed around the polished wood floors.

How did a man end up by himself with a machine that printed words, words that added up to sentences then stories?

Why did this man feel like doing this every day?

Perhaps the writing was an excuse to simply be alone, a good excuse.

It wasn't about writing but the cocoons it made.

"Stand," the writer muttered. "Or sit a little, if you can."

Mack looked at the floor, the only place to sit.

He remained standing.

"You probably feel, um, a little aimless?" said the man, head still down, keys clicking.

"Yes," Mack replied. "Aimless."

"It appears a little from your face that you are not eating."

"You haven't even looked at me."

"Little one, I looked at you, from your hair to your shoe sole."

Typing with just one hand, the writer reached into his nun's habit and pulled out a wad of bills.

"Here," he said, nudging the money and finally, really, looking at him. "Take this for a little food."

Mack took the money, shrugging. How did he know? Mack did need food.

The typing stopped. "Tell me about your big world."

"The dead girl..."

"**Another** little dead girl?" tsked the writer.

"You knew her. She had been writing to you. I saw it on some papers, then the ink disappeared."

"She had written *to me?*"

"Yes. But it's uncertain how I was with her. I just don't know how I found the body."

"You were with the dead?"

"I was."

"And you can't remember much before or after?"

"That's right," admitted Mack.

"Anything else happen?"

"A punch."

"Did it go a little crunch?"

"Yes."

"Ah, I like the crunch sound because I can use the little crunch word!"

The two men looked at each other, the small man in the chair behind his typewriter, the large man looming over him.

Mack guessed that he liked this little famous fellow after all and that the writer liked Mack; it was affection never expressed but present.

Necessarily, this writer made him think about the novelist.

"Crunch!" said the writer and squeezed his two hands into fists like an excited boy.

This made Mack smile.

"I wonder where crunch came from. It is yum on my little tongue."

"I like the word too."

"Crunch!"

Crunch, Mack thought as he left the building and found himself on the street again, counting the money the man had given him.

He saw a girl and she saw him.

No girl wants you to follow her, only to give the illusion that you can.

Her glance has to be a fast one, enough allure to gain the needed attention of his eyes.

Mack decided to follow her anyway, waiting a bit for her to pass, amused by the way she gazed briefly at him, slightly scared that he might take her up on her coy ocular offer.

For several blocks he remained behind her.

Losing interest he turned and headed back to Union Square.

CHAPTER TEN
A Body

When he came into the apartment, not hit this time, he noticed Chloe on the floor and knew she was very drunk again.

Chloe.

She was an ache in him.

The ache was a masculine wish for beauty when it never existed up close.

Never love the beautiful.

Avoid sweet skin.

Chloe, on the floor again. How many times?

He walked right past her and found Arm hungry with an empty bowl.

Thankfully, Chloe had brought him that cat food earlier.

Hadn't he already fed her?

Did cats eat every day?

He filled the bowl, the brown star pieces clinking on the metal as they poured from the bag.

Mack wanted to say something to his prostrate companion about her perpetual dipsomania, and yet this was nothing new.

Smelling salmon, he rolled up the cat food bag and stared down at his *girlfriend*, very loose on the terminology there.

When was the last time they had done anything when they slept together?

Going on a year now?

He kind of preferred the homeless shelter.

"Chloe!" he half-yelled in a whisper.

Standing over her, he put one foot on her stomach and raised a hand in mock victory. "And the winner of the relationship is...Mack Harris!!! Roaring crowd, lots of clapping, award acceptance."

Mack had passed out many times to find Chloe doing this same thing above him.

At least they kept some humor about their abject drinking.

However, her stomach did not give this time.

It was hard like marble.

Even through his shoe, this could be felt.

He pressed a bit harder as his skin prickled with fear.

He took his foot away.

She was not alive.

He knew so without even bending down to her.

But the dead girls never died.

They stayed in him and lived more than if they had remained alive.

How did the dead do it, stay in you when they were no longer there?

Memory subsumed the dead person, even magnified her.

CHAPTER ELEVEN
The Next Day

The next day, whatever that was (could have been three days of sleep; he didn't know), the next *time* he was awake, he sat up in bed and Arm came to him with a purring body sliding under his palm.

There were razor slits covering his arms.

He stared at the cuts and wondered about them, as he imagined them to be tiny undulating mouths speaking at him, hundreds of hungry baby birds wanting food.

Walking naked through the apartment, he didn't want to live, felt inertia pulling him to stop, stop all the repetitious chores, the endless eating, the needs that never quit.

I can't, he thought.

Can't even find the energy to dress.

When did I last brush my teeth?

He ran the tip of his tongue along the top of his gums and they tasted of copper and blood.

The body could stupidly soldier through living, never at a full one-hundred percent, mostly running at fifty.

What was this insistence on living, only to end?

He had to avoid going near Chloe.

Mack looked at his Bible and thought about the last time he had been in a church.

He liked to try the door of each one he saw, usually finding all of them open during the day, and he would sit inside with a daunting loneliness as the hard pew caused aches in his lower back.

He wanted to talk to someone but not the godly invisible.

He talked to himself enough.

No spirits could help him.

He was faithless, a negative Buddhist, living in each awful moment when he actually wished that he could escape into an imaginary friend like the Christmas god.

Often, Mack would find himself in a memory, a memory of opening churches, for example, and his mind would go back to each time his hand tried a door, but what happened to him in these recollections was a sort of hypnosis, a daze mesmerizing him with pictures of his past self.

An actual video camera in the corner would merely record a naked man waking and suddenly stopping in the middle of his room for hours at a time.

A video camera in the corner of his head, however, would capture preponderate thoughts moving slowly.

Today, it was the churches.

All the churches he had tried to visit when he felt empty, only to feel emptier once he was in them.

Was it the emptiness attached to these visits that led to his inner paracosm, which in turn became a physical paralysis?

In other words, was it the barrage of similar memories (churches herein) that fascinated him internally and crippled him externally?

Or was it just a revisiting of the solitude that had led him to try the doors in the first place?

In his submission to memory, he gave in to the loneliness attached to it.

Ha!

Maybe, he was trying to separate the memory from the loneliness.

Perhaps *that* was the paralysis.

At this thought, he unfroze and noticed that he was naked.

It was chilly and he shivered when it hit him, so he pulled on some sweats and a white v-neck t-shirt.

Going to the espresso maker was life. Blackness pushing through nothingness to achieve a liquid, even-more-amazing blackness was something Mack, in the repetition of tasks, stared at in awe. After he would grind the beans (crunch!), the result was always perfect crema. It was a fiercely bitter and good start to his day when he could afford the coffee beans. Thankfully, Chloe had bought some.

White cup, black substance, brown crema. How did this magic, redoubtable process invigorate him when no person could, each sip vivifying what the night killed?

And the night murdered with distracting and lucubrative dreams, did it not? Playing with coffee beans was the only adult equivalent to the messy sandbox, the clean/dirty place where cats shat, where you could firmly place yourself as a child. Grinding beans inevitably spilled espresso powder all over the white kitchen counter tiles, and he felt the need to clean it. You never had to clean a sandbox.

But then, hours later, he would still be dabbing away the flecks of coffee, like squirming fleas, his eyes one inch from the counter, peering into the grout. Often, an entire morning would be spent in this fashion. Only about four hours later would he realize what he was doing, as if a switch in him was on a delay and would click.

Red rage ensued, self-anger causing him to bite holes in his lips, repeated gashes that didn't even hurt.

He knew that he was wasting his time, but he couldn't stop himself from doing it.

And his delayed cognizance made him feel stupid to the core.

It occurred to him that maybe five shots of espresso were not a good idea for someone as obsessive as he was.

He desperately needed cold wind on him and found himself wandering, where, he was not certain.

A fever filled his face with blood, too warm, and the wind was akin to a freezing bath, ice rubbed directly onto his eyes.

The effect was that Mack almost sighed.

He walked the streets alone, again, alone.

A young girl with yellow eyes stopped right in front of him.

"Give me your phone number," she challenged him, "so I can put it in my phone."

"Why?"

"Just give it to me."

"I can't remember the number."

"You have coffee grounds all over your face," she said, pointing to his nose.

For his size, Mack was never surprised by short people who confronted him, for they had something to prove in introducing themselves.

"Coffee?"

"Yes, you look as though you rubbed coffee on your face."

"Thanks for telling me," Mack said, sheepishly recollecting his cleaning moment with the espresso granules.

"Number?"

"Oh."

For some reason, Mack gave it to her.

"I'll call you," she proclaimed like a Roman certain of Jesus' death.

Mack trotted away from her, staring back, a hyena guiltily leaving the carcass of a dead crow on the roadside.

He hadn't done anything and was still drenched in guilt.

The crowds poured on him in horizontal liquid, a tunnel of water bodies streaming past his skulking frame.

He thought of himself as a raccoon that he once saw at the ocean's shore, knowing the animal was lost or desperate, an incongruous presence.

Swarms of voices were the worst; no one voice emerged; all could be heard together, fustian one moment, tergiversation the next.

He sometimes heard the one voice of a plangent God, though, and would ask, "What do I do?"

It was only after he asked this saddened deity to help him that Mack could keep going.

He had to ask.

No other voice answered.

He acceded that it was not really God.

Still, he had to ask to be clear.

As he ran down the street looking behind him, he almost ran into two small men, one albino with red eyes, one espresso black with opaque cataract eyes.

They blocked him, refused to let him pass. He nearly toppled them but luckily had not been running too fast. Once his panting slowed, he stared at them for a moment.

They eyed him.

He had seen them many times for many years, these strange rabbit people.

Detectives.

Or so they called themselves.

His competition.

They both pulled out their badges and flashed them.

The albino was called Van.

The African was known as Trunk.

They dogged Mack.

He hated them.

Usually, when a dead girl appeared in his life, Van and Trunk showed up soon afterward.

"My, my," said the albino Van. "Mack Harris running from something. What a surprise."

"Yeah," Trunk added, pretend-sniffing around Mack's body odor. "Whew-wee. Whew-wee, my friend."

"I'm busy, you rodents."

"Rodents!" Van screamed.

"Hey," said Trunk, "didn't he just call us rodents?"

"Ain't a rodent like a rat?"

"Yes," Mack assured them. "A rodent is a rat."

"So ya go around finding dead girls," Van said, "then when the law shows, ya get leery? That the picture?"

"I'm not scared of you predictable twerpettes," Mack challenged them.

Trunk: "Why you running then?"

Van: "Wouldn't be cuz of that girl ya found dead?"

Mack: "What do you mean?"

Trunk: "Or maybe TWO girls dead."

Van: "Chloe. Ain't that your girl?"

Trunk: "Ain't she dead too? That makes two."

"Too makes two," Van said, snorting with laughter.

The two crouched over and had to put their hands on their thighs to brace themselves from a fit of giggling.

Everything they did seemed parallel.

They bent over the same.

They both placed their hands on their thighs.

Their laughing sounded similar, like cow manure splattering on the grass, laughing that was a hissing squish.

Mack was certain something was wrong.

Nothing was *this* juxtaposed in reality.

People only mimicked each other in musicals.

Life had no choreographed sense; it was certainly not iambic.

Mack tapped on the bridge of his nose with a knuckle like Morse code.

Maybe this would make them disappear.

He tapped harder, the knuckle coming faster.

Trunk and Van stood with their tiny mouths open in o's.

"Oooookay, bah, bah, bah. Okaaaaay."

Blood splashed around his eyes, rain on a windshield.

"Mack, don't hit yourself, buddy. We just playing."

"Yeah, man, ya hurting yaself."

"That's some real blood, I think."

Coming to attention like a soldier, he felt the pain that should have synapsed minutes ago. He straightened his body, stuck his tongue out at the small men, then he ran down Manhattan streets, turning, hiding and catching his breath there, ending up finally at a church, which he finally, finally entered.

But his inanition had caught up with him, hunger killing his vitality along with a minatory emptiness ravaging his core. There was a hole in his stomach, another in his thoughts. He braced himself on a pew, smelling its varnish, and he remained dizzy for a few seconds as the two holes converged.

The blood drooled down his face as if his eyes were mouths.

CHAPTER TWELVE
A Church

Inside St. Joseph's, he was calmed. The capacity of space to render him serene never failed to shock him. Why didn't he just live <u>here</u>? He walked down the aisle to the altar and saw a blue, yellow and red pietà painted on a triptych of stained glass windows, Mary holding her crucified son.

He thought of the dead girl's pills. And reddened blue eyes.

He went to a knee, still tapping the bridge of his nose with his knuckle, though softer now.

He did not want to hurt himself in this moment because he was conscious of God being in actual proximity to him.

"God?" he tried, joining his hands behind his lower back.

There was no answer.

No one had ever seen God. He knew this.

But there were some voices. These were real. These had to be people, not noises in his mind.

Mack stood and followed the sound.

A person spoke.

Hands clapped.

He walked down stairs and hugged himself from the chilliness.

It was so cold in his body and there was blood all over his hands and in his eyes.

He looked for a sign that said MEN. Next thing he knew, he was at a sink and seeing himself in a mirror. The blood was graphic, a modern painting of a face. He did not have the energy to wipe it away. Within the blood were the grains of the espresso beans he had ground earlier.

Blood and coffee.

He neologized a portmanteau: bloffee.

Coflood.

Neologisms made him smile.

Outside the men's room, he could go could left or right.

He went left.

Left he went down an empty hall, still hearing voices that he knew were not unreal.

And then he found them.

A stunning fluorescence blinded him as a balding man with white hair gazed his way.

"Come in, friend," he said, motioning.

There was only one other woman in the room. She was elderly with neon blue hair like cotton candy, and she stared into the distance toward a wall, her eyes slightly crossed.

"What is this?" Mack asked.

"Come in," the man said again.

"Zechariah says," the woman began, "'What is to die, let it die.'"

"Yes," the kind man said, nodding, fingering the onion pages of his Bible.

Mack sat at the end of the table, and the man told him his eyes were bleeding. Mack said he knew that he was covered with blood but that he could not help it. The man asked Mack if he needed help, was he all right?

Mack wondered how he ended up in places with strangers all the time.

Would he ever be in a room with his family again, with people who knew him?

Or would he be doomed to the strange?

Was it, in fact, doom?

Strangers loved him and looked after him.

They offered a propriety that family did not.

He could not even remember his family, except for a brother, Ford, who taught in a college in New York State. He had been meaning to visit him for long time. Never did.

"What are you reading?" asked Mack.

"We are doing the Synoptics, Matthew, Mark and Luke."

"The Synoptics?"

Suddenly, the woman screamed, a long scream. To this point, she had not seen Mack's face. Her eyes were now lucidly focused on him. Mack listened to this shriek that was palpable as sex. He stared at the man. The shriek would not stop. It paused the room. She covered her mouth, she stood, she ran from them. Mack watched her as she fled.

It was just he and the man, the wake of the scream still rippling around the emptiness. There is nothing like the vacancy of sound after a scream.

"I'm sorry about that," said the man.

"No...my appearance, it must scare everyone."

"I'm not scared. I can tell you are trying to find something. You are not unkind. Maybe unlucky. But a sweet boy nonetheless."

A sweet boy? When had he last been a sweet boy?

"Please sit."

The old man handed him a folded white handkerchief and suggested that he wipe his face. Mack took the padded square of white linen and examined it.

"A gift," the man told him.

"What are the Synoptics?" Mack inquired, but didn't wipe away the blood. He put the handkerchief back on the table.

"Well, as I said, they are the three parallel texts of Matthew, Mark and Luke. Synoptic means *one eye*."

"One eye," Mack said to himself. "And who are you?"

"I am Theo Seneg."

"How did I get here?"

"Well, some would say that you knew you should be here."

"I don't know anything. My mind won't tell things apart anymore."

"Yes," said Theo, "yes, I understand."

Morse code, on the chin, on the nose, on the chin, on the nose. "I thought I would see God today."

"Hard to see, sometimes."

"Yes."

"Take my handkerchief. Wipe that blood. I have to go see about that woman who was just here."

"I upset her with my appearance."

"It's fine. Will you do something for me?"

"Of course. You helped me. I would like to help you, if I possibly can."

"Please recognize who you are."

"How do you mean?" Mack asked.

"You cannot pretend anymore."

"About myself?"

"That's right."

"How do you know who I am?"

"Mack Harris, you are well-known to many. You must try to be well-known to yourself."

"It's not my fault," Mack tried.

"I don't think that's completely true."

"Then what?"

"I don't know, but you must try more than you have."

"I will. I will try."

"You can't force trying, if it isn't true."

"Nothing ever seems true anymore."

"Yes, that is it, nothing is true."

Theo rose and gave him a tender smile, patting him on the shoulder as he left.

Mack Harris.

Again, alone.

CHAPTER THIRTEEN
An Uncomfortable Office

All offices were sterile and unhuman to Mack Harris. Sanitized fakery with yeasty people (who always managed to maintain these jobs) having power over him, sign this, do this, check in here.

This office he knew.

It was a pre-office, the small office before the big office where he had to sit like a punished dunce-of-a-child, only to be escorted by the little-office dimwit secretary with large teeth into the big-office of his psychiatrist (who, oddly, had small teeth).

He didn't even know how he remembered the weekly visits, and yet he always showed up to them, some internal temporal inculcation that lured him back to the hollowness of being a patient.

Wasn't it true that psychiatrists truly had no reason for their patients to heal, though, since healing meant the stopping of payment? In the end, insanity was an ongoing market and while he hated being a psychological slug who needed this, he also knew that it was impossible to escape from the group.

The group of humans he loathed.

He was one of them, one of the worst even, meaning that if he hated them, he, by default, had to hate himself, a pretender of individuality.

He was simply not an individual.

My god, he needed this psychiatrist, this educated idiot with a beard who merely listened, never proselytized, just listened. All he did was listen! As if listening was some potently aural and paramount skill. Listening was the opposite of selfish humans, and to pretend to listen was counter, absolutely counter to people's desire to talk about themselves.

Mack's chest ached and he couldn't breathe. These thoughts made him feel awful. He knew he was right, but being right made you terrible. Speaking the truth was electrifying, the freedom, but it horribly electrocuted you at the same time. Mack thought, in this moment, in the small waiting room that *electrify* and *electrocute* had some genius in them, could possibly be godful.

His legs would not stop moving.

He sensed the hairs on his beard growing, pushing out from the skin of his face, the itching, my god the itching.

He rubbed his face; did he even have a beard?

Yes, he did.

And the hairs were now as long and thick as spaghetti.

I am right here but losing me, once more.

"Mack Harris. He will see you now."

Mack, like a drunk, which he was not, stood and walked like a drunk pretending to be semi-sober.

And though he thought he was spinning, he knew he wasn't.

He walked from the small office to the big office, a beard greeting him before the body.

He stood in the doorjamb.

He sighed.

His psychiatrist sighed.

They were tired of each other.

But they loved the presence of madness in each.

It was duel.

It was Samurai.

It was cerebral high noon.

It was nothing physical.

Only two silly, deep, sorry, futile heads, meeting we(a)(e)kly.

"Whew, hello Mack, you're killing me, you know. People leave when they see you in the waiting room. You have to bathe! I've lost some patients."

"What, Botoxed divorcees whose biggest fear is a bad playdate?"

"Those women occasionally suffer."

"Rich women never suffer because they keep colorful dildos in their underwear drawers. They are entitled pseudo-queens, lost in the vitriol of ex-husbands they never divorce but are always connected to because of their kids. And we all know their ex-husbands were dicks to begin with. Please."

"Mack, ha, well, I can't laugh. You speak some truth."

"Psychiatrists are politicians. Speaking of killing," Mack replied to this nonsense, changing the vapid subject, "I have killed again."

"You're on repeat."

"No, this time I think I killed. Twice!"

"Mack."

The psychiatrist touched his shoulder, reached up.

"You are not a killer. You are a head-killer. You kill in your head, okay? We all kill in our head. It's hard not to. I kill in my head. But, look, I tell you the same thing all the time. I do. And, I guess, I know you will never get it, and, gosh, maybe that's why you come here, so I shouldn't judge you, oh, I wish, I could shake you. You are just in a fugue, nothing else, you have absented yourself, come back!"

Mack loved the psychiatrist. He was optimism. He was bright. He was not dark, although a dark night was peaceful.

The novelist was dark. He was more Mack's speed. He needed to do mushrooms with the novelist. The novelist kept asking him to join in this experience. Why waste time on the fake? The fake was in all things: traffic, lawyers, doctors, accountants, bankers.

In short, all the great fake jobs earned you great fake women, for most men had these jobs and most women bought into garnering them.

Mack's utopia would be when fakery was subsumed by some honest questions and women stopped accepting monkeys for mates.

He digressed.

His head throbbed, a foot pedal slapping on a bass drum.

In the end, Mack guessed he needed the novelist and the psychiatrist in both respects.

The novelist spoke truth no one wanted to hear because it was so accurate; the psychiatrist had emotions Mack had forgotten.

God, were the novelist and the psychiatrist conjoined twins?

The novelist: a poor man's psychiatrist.

The psychiatrist: a rich man's novelist.

Too easy.

"Mack, you are pulling your beard hair. Stop."

Mack stopped.

He listened when he could, when listening matched up to his head.

He was here in Sam's office with many windows, clear urban paintings.

He stared out on the city, out of the psychiatrist's window and he just couldn't understand anything.

The buildings loved him.

Hell, the window was lucid.

"Sam." This was the doctor's name, right? Was he using the right name? God, he forgot names all the time.

It was Sam. He knew it to be Sam.

"Mack, I've missed you."

"And I you."

"But what is wrong?"

"Jesus, Sam, I am not the novelist!"

"No, not true."

"No, I am, I am."

"Take my hand, Mack, okay?"

Mack looked at Sam's green eyes and took his hand. In truth, he touched the hairs on Sam's hands and examined them. The hair on a hand, human cilia waving in wind like wheat swaying. He couldn't stand it, the small things. The small things made him grimace.

"Mack, what's wrong? How is your new novel coming?"

"I think," he said, staring at the small hairs, "that I have forgotten everything."

Sam let go.

"And," Mack went on, "I don't know if I killed two people. I don't know."

Sam covered his mouth.

"I need you to follow me," Mack instructed him.

"Okay, I am listening."

"I have no ability to know the difference."

"The difference between what?" asked Sam.

"The difference between anything. Can you keep a Synoptic eye on me?"

"I can. Where are the bodies?"

Mack told him addresses and left suddenly, remembering that Sam had asked him about *his* new novel?!

CHAPTER FOURTEEN
Mack Meandering in Brutum Fulmen
(Irrational Thunderbolts)

Mack rushed onto the street and like a plow dug through the people, the dirt of the city.

He needed to find the novelist.

He was sure the psychiatrist would be following him after that conversation.

They would *all* be chasing him soon.

Chasser. Middle French for "to hunt".

The hunt had been in the chase from the beginning.

Why did you chase a person if not to hunt him?

He thought of himself as a plow, his face spreading the people/dirt, knocking them out of the way with his wide shoulders.

He despised the city because he was the city.

His identity was only urban and yet he ached for the rural.

What if it was that easy, that people were dirt and he could plow them up as he pleased?

He was not a plow.

He had never seen a farm.

People were not dirt, though they were.

Suddenly, he had bumped into Chloe.

Or she had stopped him.

He didn't know.

Chloe?

"Hi Mackie."

"But..."

"I have an eye audition, got to run."

And she was gone.

He looked at her as she skipped off.

He knew whom he needed to see next.

. . .

He felt that he had been here already.

"Come in, come in, make sure not to spin."

The little man again.

"I need advice," Mack said, uneasily.

"Crunch!" he said, clapping his hands together and leaving them this way.

"I want to ask a question, and the question is this: what if I say *squish* when you say *crunch*?"

"Oh yes, squish when I crunch. I like it a bunch."

"I just saw Chloe."

"Of course you did. She came here to hear me crunch!"

"She did?"

"Yes, yes, but you forgot say squish as you had wished."

"Right. Squish."

"And she came here for you because she loves your hairdo."

"She does?"

"Crunch yes she does!"

"Oh my squish," Mack muttered. "But Chloe dislikes me too."

"True, Mack, love is endlessly disliking someone."

"It is."

"No more crunching for a moment. Which means no more squishing. You, Mack, um, er, well, hmm. You are going to be beheaded by yourself one day. Maybe you think this is impossible, but that's how I see it."

"I will cut my own head off?" Mack said, moving closer.

"I think so. I figured it out three hours ago while clipping my nose hairs, collecting them and applying them above my lip to create this fake mustache I made."

"I noticed the mustache."

"However, it is merely nose hairs glued there."

"Do you mean this literally, about the beheading?"

"Yes. I'm afraid so. Still, I think it could be a small part of your head, maybe not from the neck, perhaps only from the eyeballs upward."

"That sounds an awful lot like a lobotomy," Mack informed him.

"Indeed. Whatever, it's something with your head, okay? I was talking to God about it and that's what S/HE said. It might also be that I was so focused on my new mustache that misheard H/ER/IM. So there could be a linguistical play, such as 'Mack could *be heading* down a bad road.' I misheard God!! Sorry."

"Don't worry about it. I think it would be complicated to behead myself and they don't do many lobotomies anymore. Maybe it's the *be heading* thing."

"Mayyyyyyybe, or it might just be time again to go *crunch*."

Mack rushed into the streets again and saw the psychiatrist immediately at a hot dog stand, pretending not notice him.

Mack felt his body jog then run then sprint then gasp for air.

God was talking to the little man, and the damn little man was not even listening!

Now Chloe was the undead, the psychiatrist was never going to stop examining him and he still needed to find the novelist.

Plus, someone had hit him recently.

Who had hit him?!

He had to find out who had done that to him.

The dead girl: he had nearly forgotten her.

Of course, these were the least of his worries because Trunk, the African, and Van, the albino, stepped out of nowhere and tripped him, each with a foot. They had been waiting.

As his head spiraled down to the sidewalk, he thought of the little man's beheading oracle, especially when his forehead smacked the concrete with nothing else to break the fall.

And it would not be so easy as to simply faint.

No, Mack would lie face down, his head bleeding, his mind thinking and all of him feeling each part of the pain in him with vivid, red anguish.

CHAPTER FIFTEEN
The Undead

He stayed down on the sidewalk for a long time; in fact, he slept there for what felt like a few days and maybe those days became a week.

People walked over him as if he were a crack on the concrete.

He moved finally to a corner away from the foot traffic.

His body had quit caring and his mind no longer challenged how he felt. It simply mixed too many thoughts together, a juggling of chainsaws.

In this sense, he sighed in resignation to many different kinds of pain, the pains of fists, the pains of an empty heart, the pains of loss, the pains of confusion in his head never aligning with reality.

A few nights on the street helped him think.

Here, he was a leper.

No one hated him.

Indeed, each person who passed by his body feared him or, moreover, feared *becoming* him.

It was comic, their false respect.

Thank goodness I am not him, they were thinking.

Funnily enough, this was the most privacy he had felt in a long time with all these feet and legs stumbling by his face, his cheek on the concrete, concrete that was cold all night and warm all day.

What did he need to do?

He pulled out a small notebook and decided the answer had to be with the people he already knew:

The little crunch man. Or the little man crunch. He never knew what to call him.

Chloe.

Oscar, her ex.

Van and Trunk.

The dead girl.

The novelist.

Sam, his psychiatrist.

As he wrote, the writing scribbled itself, the pencil moving.

All the pedestrians had frozen.

He could only stare at the pencil writing by itself, no hands.

Then his hand was in control again, the legs moving past him, the pencil in his control.

"My gosh," the little crunch man said to him, bending over Mack. "What has happened here?"

"They tripped me, the other detectives."

"Oh yes, your *supposed* competition."

"Yes," Mack admitted. "They are competitive."

"Crunch them forever."

"Yes, I'll crunch them," Mack agreed.

"Will you finally ever be okay?"

"My legs can't move."

"What?"

"I can't move my legs."

"Should I call the ambulance?"

"No, no need."

"Maybe, you *won't* move your legs. Maybe you like it down there where it's easy to never go lower."

"Maybe."

"I think it's true. You can move your legs."

"Possibly."

"Have you gone to the bathroom? How long have you been here?"

Mack thought before he answered.

It had certainly felt like three days, a week, but he had not soiled himself.

"I just fell. An hour ago."

"Mack, we will have to crunch some bad people, won't we?"

"Yes. I don't know where to start."

"Ah, we will start with your getting up."

Mack, for some reason, stood.

"Then we will proceed to create many crunches."

The little crunch man was right.

First, though, he had to go back to the dead girl.

CHAPTER SIXTEEN
The Novelist Absolutely Needs to Interrupt Here

It seems to me that when I write about Mack, he subsumes himself, forgetting the narrative.

We have a complicated character here.

He makes us ask a lot of questions.

Is he serious?

Does he see what he sees?

Or can he not be trusted?

Why does he sound so right all the time?

Why do we believe him, or is it the fact that we know he is insane, are fascinated by it, and realize, perhaps, that insanity sounds correct sometimes?

If you are asking these questions, you probably feel the same about Mack as I do.

As I mentioned, he is a real person, not a character.

This is the trickiest part of all, convincing you that I know him, and that all I'm doing is reportage, journalizing about Mack.

There is no fiction, only conveying of narratives that I was lucky enough to see.

I know we need a break from Mack.

I need a break from him.

I never don't love him.

He just takes everything I have.

At some point, I hope to make you empathize with the novelist.

Right now, this is for Mack.

Narratives *can* unfold with some foresight, yes, but there is also backsight (also known as endsight), which is what occurs when the foresight has run its course.

In other words, a writer can architect a story, but when a character takes over, this is known as backsight.

Bad writers refuse to let the character backsight happen, holding on to the authorial foresight.

Good writers know when it is time to let their characters possess their backsight.

CHAPTER SEVENTEEN
Back to the Dead Girl

With the little man crunch, Mack wanted to find his way back to the dead student's room in an attempt to re-examine the girl he had discovered in recent days.

He took the homunculus, a writer, as a witness perhaps to record what Mack was seeing.

Although he wished it was the novelist, the little man crunch would do.

The psychiatrist was not far behind them either, even though Mack could not see him.

He *felt* him.

And Van and Trunk were behind the psychiatrist.

He felt them too.

He had dreamed of this chase many nights, an extended hounding that might last for days, not quite a posse, but a series of people following him, targeting him.

For years, he dreamed of being chased like this, individual people separated by minor distances, yet all deciding to converge on Mack Harris with simultaneity.

A posse was a faction with a mission.

This was not a faction.

It was every "enemy" he thought he had, deciding to pick on him, coincidentally, without consulting each other.

But it made sense, for Mack had not really dreamed this, only sensed its verity.

That he was not able to recapitulate it out of the dream into the real (until now) made sense; it was not supposed to happen until now.

Now, he could recap.

He had two friends: 1) the novelist and 2) the little man crunch.

And Chloe was alive.

He didn't have to worry about her now.

Often, we are utterly deluded about those with whom we live.

They become hated habits.

In reflection, though, hated habits turn into nostalgic reasons to keep people around we despise.

There was comfort in despising.

It was that: comfort.

He despised her, Chloe, then she comforted him as he glanced at her eyelashes.

In this thoughtful moment, he felt at ease with her.

There were others that concerned him.

To give his mind peace, he ran into a restaurant, found a napkin and came back outside to the sidewalk.

On the napkin he circumscribed a poor circle, more of an oval, an ellipse even, but to him it was a circle.

He drew spokes, radii, and on each spoke/radius he wrote things that centered him, things that did not.

He wrote "the little man crunch" on one of the spokes/radii, and pointed an arrow toward the center, the arrow meaning that this little man moved him toward the center, centered him.

But he wrote "Van and Trunk" on another and pointed an arrow outward, indicating these two moved him **away** from center.

He wanted to be the dot in the center of a circle, not the arcs on the perimeter.

Arcs meant he was uncentered.

The dot meant he was in the absolute middle, the geometric perfection of centeredness.

He would never get there.

So the chase was not a line!

It was not, say, all of his enemies running after him in a protracted line, but it was a circle of lines (radii), some of which were pointed positively to the center, some pointed negatively to the outer arcs.

Yes, he had his delusions.

Yes, he knew the other dead girl was what he had to follow.

The cases kept him sane.

But he was inside the circle of those chasing him.

Somehow the comfort of knowing that his paranoia was contained within a circle gave it (the paranoia) limits.

A line could stretch on forever.

Whew, Mack breathed.

A circle.

I have been seeing things in one long line.

Now it's a finite circle with finite radii.

There are many chases within those radii; I know this.

But I *see* the circle.

I see that I am simplistically finite.

Moreover, I can stop thinking in one long line of people chasing me forever.

The circle gives me relief.

I cannot handle lines that do not end.

I can handle that I am chased within circularity.

Manhattan!

It was a tall circle. He was right in it, autochthonous and urban.

The little man crunch gawped at him as he scratched a circle on a napkin kneeling on a Bleecker Street sidewalk.

Mack was onto an aetiology in his fractured self.

When you had a nascent recognition, you had to stop and let it come to you.

The little man crunch was worried at first.

Then he nodded.

He had waited for Detective Harris to come away from his despondent, scabrous self that had never known more than semi-epiphany filtered through lunacy.

Now, Mack had concretized it, irrefragably.

It was bouleversement, tossing out an edacious soul.

Crunch!

The dead girl would have to wait.

For two hours, Mack drew circles on his napkin, which led to his creating lapidary circles on the sidewalk.

Drawing them with a pen was not easy.

Each circle was similar, the same radii, the same arrows pointing in and out, who would center him, who would be inimical or mephitic.

The little man crunch withheld his crunching since Mack was touching on sanity.

It was a tremblingly sad time for the little man because he knew these instances were so rare.

When the lost are able to see, it is one of the untouchables.

Stand back.

Let it occur.

Mack would rise.

He would be moving forward soon to the dead girl.

Let him draw circles with a pen that could barely etch his wish.

CHAPTER EIGHTEEN
Clarification

Mack tells me that my writing is a wall of sorts, which is why I reach out to him, a man who would otherwise meander in psychosis, having no voice without me.

He regrets that I have found no one while also believing that my writing exile has brought me to him.

Mack firmly believes that my aloneness allows me to tell his story.

In ways, he is right.

He also thinks Chloe is his girlfriend when she is mine.

I let him think so.

We are lemniscated, an infinity sign, that sideways eight, two ribbons conjoined in the infinite.

How a sideways eight equals infinity, I will never understand (because it looks finite to me), but I see us, Mack and me, as each side of that lemniscated symbol.

For example, we are not a cross; it doesn't fit.

We are an infinity symbol, two sides.

Whew, I am supposed to be clear.

I'm just fogging the narrative here like cold breath on a winter window.

Let's get back to Mack and the chase of his life.

We left Mack with the little man crunch on the street.

Mack was drawing circles, devolving the former limits of his linear chase.

A circle was forming, and Mack's cognizance of it was enough to arrest the literary little man crunch into a momentary submission of respect.

Little man crunch.

Mack drawing circles on the sidewalk.

Set this scene:

City place.

Two men you would ignore for simply being one of many urbanly normal freaks.

Narrative is resistance.

The erotic is the same, minus darkness.

How much longer will Mack Harris resist what he had simply wanted as a boy: to get the image in his head to match up with the body in front of him?

Mack stops the circles, halting abruptly feeling a parlous tension.

He runs, sensing peril.

The little man crunch follows.

Behind them:

The psychiatrist runs.

Van and Trunk keep coming.

And what's this?

Is this the novelist running after his own characters?

Could it be the point at which the novelist realizes he can't just have drinks with Mack, a character he made, a character he is trying to convince others to believe is real?

Come on novelist!

Sure, run after him.

He's the best thing for your fiction you could never imagine yourself.

Mack is real, though. I've told you this.

But the chase has encircled itself in enclosed linearity.

We have been waiting for the novelist to finally realize that Mack is not real.

We have a serious chase.

We have some contradictory narratives.

Chloe is the novelist's girlfriend. True or false?

True.

Mack Harris *is* a novelist and *has* written a book.

True.

The novelist across the hall does not exist.

True.

Mack forgets that he is a famous writer.

True.

The novelist across the hall is writing this book.

False.

Is this book fiction?

No, it is real.

Is there a dead girl?

We don't know that yet. We may never know.

Follow the hunt.

Are Mack and the novelist the same person?

Yes.

A narrative is a hunting, a merging of prey and posse.

As we are seeing, narrative is pukka; narration is rendered nugatory.

CHAPTER NINETEEN
Lure

Mack knew that time itself, because he rarely had a sense of it, was his real antagonist.

Many people were after him, some people, some characters.

Damned novelist! He had convoluted Mack's head into a frenetic wire sculpture of fiction and non-fiction.

Did it matter if the people/characters after him were fictive/non-fictive?

Yes and no.

But there it was.

He was being chased by the real and the not real.

That he didn't know the difference was partially his fault, partly the novelist's encouragement.

See, the novelist lived across the hallway (or did he?) and pretended to care about Mack.

Maybe he did care.

But he also used Mack for his fiction.

Mack was real, to himself, and Mack was fiction, to the novelist.

It wasn't a question of not knowing himself.

He knew this bifurcation well.

After he was tripped, though, his moiety, as a character, and his moiety, as a person, became one.

Who was hunting him?

He knew the chasers.

Ah.

It was irrelevant since he was being chased.

The Buddhists had a concept, shenpa, attachment, focusing too much on what you can't control.

He focused on the fact that he was overfocusing and realized that a phalanx was in pursuit.

Worrying was bootless.

As he ran, for he was sprinting and out of breath, he did not look behind him but only saw the real and the unreal in his head.

This was another moment of pause.

It was not as if the chase was in his mind; it was.

It was not as if there were unreal characters coming for him; they were.

What it was, was this: he was running in/from/within/by/near/without/on/with his head.

Any preposition would work here.

His own thoughts tailed him, just as the fiction being written about him merged with his cognizance that being written about was tantamount to being chased.

When it occurred to him that he was also the co-author (and maybe the author), well, he just decided to run faster.

He could not handle this backsight.

He could not believe that he was the same person as the novelist.

CHAPTER TWENTY
*The Novelist Admits He Is
Chasing Mack Harris
While Also Trying to
Write a Chase Scene
With Mack Harris*

Is it surprising that I (the novelist) run after my character, Mack, who is real and also writing this book with me?

What is most paramount is that I separate myself from him while using him.

So let's gather the fictive and non-fictive facts: a character I stole from reality is being chased by the *other* characters I fabricated.

Those characters after him are obviously invented, but Mack is such a gray one in his protagonistic complexity.

He's based on someone I know; that was how he started.

Then he became a character, whom I truly separated from the real person on whom he was based.

Now, what is happening is this: Mack is developing a consciousness in which parts are fiction, parts are not.

He may not know exactly what he's thinking, but, intuitively he knows something is up.

For a novelist, you can imagine that I'm proud of my character for becoming his own person.

It's tough for a character these days.

I mean, if you think about it, a character has no parents, no childhood.

Everything is forced on him by the writer.

Now, the rest of this narrative is going to be a sell-out noir chase scene.

It's very non-literary, but I don't judge myself.

In fact, I love chase scenes.

I will admit that I do.

Going forward, let's all try to remember that Mack Harris is an orphan at heart.

He has no memory of the life before this novel.

And he's partially running from this vacant aspect of himself.

He may try to convince you that he is the novelist and that the novelist does not exist; nevertheless, you are merely inside his backsight.

How often do we run from what is not there?

In his defense, Mack is fleeing from a vanished part of himself.

Actually, that is not true.

Something has to exist before it vanishes, right?

He is running from what was never there.

As a character he has no long-term past.

His only life is this book.

His life is only short-term.

He is only a book.

He only lives when you read him.

Therefore, I have to give him life now in this chase.

And the reason he forgets that he is a writer is that I like it that way.

He helps me create, receives auctorial credit and then can't remember anything.

Does he truly co-write with me?

It's tricky to answer.

All I can say is that Mack is real and that some of the other characters are not.

Mack and I, yes, do collaborate on his stories.

You probably don't believe me at this point since you think Mack is an author, and I am not.

You sympathize with him because his schizophrenia makes you want to believe him.

However, I created him and he has developed beyond my creation; he has matured from mere character to author, a deserved promotion.

In other words, I guess the best way to express it is as such: I couldn't write *The Killer Detective Novelist* without him.

And if you haven't noticed, I don't have a name.

My name never appears on the cover, only Mack's.

It could be that Mack is right, that I am merely a part of him that he invents because he cannot deal with the writing he does.

Or could it be that I am a character of Mack's who is individuating also?

CHAPTER TWENTY-ONE

Prelude: The Longest Chase Scene in Novel History

We have been very creative to this point, taking time to play with words, juggling them around like a verbal circus act.

And we have, in effect, been writing in the purlieus of that circle Mack created, the one that quasi-ordered his thoughts.

Circle, circus, hmm, terribly homonymic.

Nevertheless all narratives are lines in the end, even though Mack thinks he is living in a distorted circle.

We are at the line part of the book.

The radii of the tall circle of Manhattan are the streets and avenues—where our characters will end this novel.

These lines will take over and diminish the outer circle.

You know all the characters.

You know Mack is unreliable in his perceptions.

You know the setting.

As Mack becomes absorbed into his earned backsight, watch also how the city turns into a character of its own.

CHAPTER TWENTY-TWO
The Longest Chase Scene in Novel History

Mack Harris turned his head to the side as he ran, noticing no one on the sidewalk anymore, except homeless men under boxes.

The little man crunch was gone; he could not keep up with his short legs.

As he sprinted up 2nd Avenue and tore muscles in his back and legs, he refused to stop.

At least the little man crunch was not after him.

Who was, though?

Was anyone?

It was night.

He had started running during the day and now it was dark.

He didn't care if he hurt himself because the end of this chase would kill him.

And he needed to not stop.

It didn't make sense that Van and Trunk would be after him.

They might threaten him, trip him, but they were legitimate detectives.

Mack was not.

He was literally unreal, fantasized by some drunk writer in a room who might even be himself.

He was not a real detective.

But they knew Mack was fiction.

Real detectives couldn't kill fictive ones.

Or could they?

His gut feeling was that Van and Trunk, while menacing, had no real beef with Mack.

Sam, his psychiatrist.

Mack had *asked* him to chase him.

Pathetic.

Trying to get a guy to chase you to make it look like a chase scene. Pfft.

Chloe was alive and apparently not even his girlfriend.

The novelist had simply used her in a few scenes with Mack, making him believe she was his.

And if the novelist had tortured Mack's head in this manner, wasn't it also possible that there was no dead girl at all?

As these thoughts occurred to him, he slowed his pace to a jog.

Then he knew.

The fist was the novelist's.

He lived across the hall.

No, correction.

He was the novelist.

The punch could have only come from within him.

Sadly, he had only passed out; there was no fist.

The novelist was after him, internally, making it look like an external conflict. There had never been a punch. He had fallen to the floor and spent so much time thinking he had been hit. It was easy to wish that the novelist was another person because it kept him from the loneliness of writing. This was good. He was the novelist. Gradual acceptance of this was coming.

Didn't he notice the novelist running after him earlier with the rest of the group?

Mack hadn't given it much thought, at first.

Oh, now it made sense.

It was the showdown they had always discussed at the bar, but it had never occurred to him that the novelist would need to murder Mack Harris.

This whole time Mack had assumed the killer would be one of the characters created along the way.

He had helped create these characters as they co-wrote them.

But the answer is usually right in front of you.

Mack stopped jogging.

He stood still.

He looked around the city.

On 2nd Avenue, he had come north to 32nd Street.

Maybe it was three a.m., maybe five a.m.

Sweat poured down his face like a veil.

A plastic page, susurrus, blew down the sidewalk.

He was doomed.

His mind went over the clear facts:

1) There was no dead girl.
2) Chloe was the novelist's girlfriend, not his. This meant she was also his girlfriend but no longer. She loved the novelist in him more than the Mack in him.
3) The little man crunch was his friend but of no use.
4) The novelist had punched him inside his head to disorient him. Why? Because Mack was becoming too in control of the narrative. The novelist within could make him believe things that were not true.

Oh my god, he thought, I can't do anything about this but just run.

Yet why am I running when I know the novelist can catch me whenever he wants?

Is there really a chase if we are the same person?

Are all chases inside of us?

Or does he just want me to *think* he's chasing me?

Whatever the case, my head is clearer.

It is no longer cluttered with illusions.

I am not a detective.

I am only a character who developed too much.

Would he kill me?

No wonder I was always pondering death.

I am on the cusp of it, refusing to truckle to the novelist's whims.

I am about to die.

* * *

Mack decided to walk and not worry about his head anymore. His previous obsession with dying now made him smile.

His earlier spurious thoughts had been delusional, rendering him nervous and confused.

He was glad they were gone.

As he turned he saw the little man crunch rolling along on a two-seater bicycle.

He braked beside Mack.

"Get on the back seat. We have to crunch."

"What, why?"

"The novelist is crunching after us."

Mack climbed on the bike and they pedaled together, synchronous, bumping over the holes in the street.

"Where did you see him?" Mack yelled up to the little man crunch.

"I didn't."

"How do you know he's after me?"

"Because I went to see Chloe and she's dead."

"She's not dead. The novelist is playing with your thoughts too. I thought she was dead, then I saw her on the street."

"Mack, she's dead. I watched him kill her."

"What?"

"He didn't know I was there."

"But how did you get there?"

"I came to see her because I was worried and I heard screaming, so I opened the door, which, for some reason was unlocked. Then I saw the most crunch thing I have ever seen. It was a gruesome strangling. The novelist saw me and I managed to dart away because he was so drunk. He fell and hurt his wrist."

"Where did you get this bike?"

"I had it parked and locked by a parking meter."

"Where are we going?"

"I don't know, Mack. I just don't crunch."

* * *

The novelist had come undone.

As they pedaled, Mack felt absurd on the tandem.

Manhattan itself was just like that oval he had drawn, the tall circle, with the streets shooting out from its center like radii.

Here he was on a bicycle, as well, with two tires, circles, radii.

The chase would be contained, for the novelist wanted it that way.

Mack could not escape.

Sure, he could usually take a train to Connecticut or New Jersey but not at this hour since they had all stopped service.

His brother, Dr. Ford Harris, in New York State? Should he call him?

The novelist had given Mack some prescient knowledge as he drew that circle.

He was really drawing Manhattan and his own self-contained urban death.

Again, the novelist had made Mack think he was in control and clearing his head.

All Mack was doing was mapping out the place of his termination.

Knowing that he could not leave Manhattan, he tried to figure out where the novelist might tree him.

But it would happen here for certain.

He knew the city where he would die.

Fitting.

He was an urban orphan.

He was about to address the little man crunch when a bizarre thing occurred.

They had been fluidly riding along in the empty night when the novelist appeared from nowhere with an ax.

The homunculus playwright's head lifted, bounced onto Mack's chest and rolled on the asphalt.

And for about another block or so, his little legs kept pedaling.

Mack stopped as soon as he realized what was happening.

As he dismounted, the little man crunch's body fell sideways, and blood sprayed up from the neck like a sprinkler.

Mack saw the guillotined head lying in the darkness.

This was when the true chase started. Dropping his ax, the novelist (with a flaccid wrist) came after Mack.

Mack, taking a last brief moment with his dead friend, stood, looked at the shadow of the novelist and began running again.

Out of absolute nowhere, a black livery cab pulled up beside him and a window whirred down.

"Mack, get in the back," Van the albino said.

Trunk was driving.

Mack opened the door quickly just as the novelist was about to catch him.

It slammed.

The tires screeched.

They drove south into the West Village and further downtown into Wall Street where Mack watched zombies slam their fists on the car window.

He stared at them and their painted faces and had never realized there were zombies in Manhattan.

The car rocked as they tried to flip them.

Mack couldn't put together the details.

One minute he was on the West Side Highway looking at the Hudson at night.

In another he was on Wall Street with the zombies.

The little man crunch had predicted his own decapitation.

There were things he needed to know.

"The novelist is after us."

"Yes," Van and Trunk spoke in unison. "He is. But we have to eat first."

CHAPTER TWENTY-THREE
An Odd Feast

At this point, the novelist no longer has the full power to interrupt, and therein is a lacuna in which Mack, Van and Trunk can grab a bite, use the restroom and figure out a plan.

There is usually a delayed reaction in narratives like these when the assumed writer doesn't receive the information immediately that he's lost control of his book.

The characters have a moment, thus, to convene and enjoy a meal without too much stress.

It only lasts for an hour or so (and pretty soon characters will no longer have this luxury with all the new technology).

Van and Trunk were unusually silent, funereal even, eyeing Mack in the back seat and knowing his time was circumscribed, delimited.

In a literary execution, you had to provide a last meal.

And so they parked and ended up at the only place in Manhattan that served one table at a time, according to Trunk.

It was on Broome at the corner of Ludlow.

Chef Sam Orion and his sous-chef Chris Two-Side emerged from behind a purple curtain and greeted them.

How, Mack thought, does a restaurant survive with one table?

"Mack Harris!" Chef Sam Orion nearly screamed.

"It is he-him," Chris Two-Side added.

"He-him is here with his writing."

"Oooh, he-him."

Mack looked at them.

"Him who is he," Chef Sam cooed.

Van and Trunk had been here before and merely stood back as Mack met the puzzling chefs.

"What do we eat here?" Mack asked, feeling stupid for asking.

"Oooh, we do not serve food," Chef Sam Orion informed him.

"Yes, we serve suggestions," Chris Two-Side said. "We are known for our suggestions."

"There's no food here?"

"Only we serve one suggestion for one person."

Mack looked at Van and Trunk with one raised eyebrow.

"And you just have this one table?"

"Yes, one table for one person to whom we give one suggestion."

For the first time in his life, Mack Harris felt saner than two people.

"You bring me here because...?" he said, opening his hands in a why.

But Van and Trunk would not speak.

Chef Sam Orion seated him at the white table with the white chair.

Chris Two-Side waited on him. "You may order your suggestion now."

"But, um, there is no menu."

"HA HA," Chef Sam Orion nearly screamed.

"Yes, oh, HA HA," Chris Two-Side repeated.

Mack was big enough to hurt them all, and yet he never wanted to bother anyone.

He sat submissively amid this absurd collocation and was done with wonder.

Wonder had murdered him; it was the worst squandering.

Time was the thing he had.

He wanted an espresso.

To pet his warm cat.

To finally have that supposedly life-changing talk with Chloe. To figure out what was real and what was not.

Maybe he did need a suggestion.

"What, um, suggestion do you recommend?"

"He-him," Chef Sam Orion said in admiration.

"You are missing the he of the him," Chris Two-Side informed Mack. "This is your suggestion."

"The he of the him?"

"Yes, we see you as the he-him," Chef Sam Orion said. "We **know** you as he-him."

"You only see you as the *him*," Chris Two-Side explained. "You are missing your he."

"The <u>he</u> of the he-him," Chef Sam Orion further explained.

"I am missing my he of my he-him?" Mack tried to clarify.

"Yes!!" they both said, clapping like a studio audience.

More shrugs from Van and Trunk.

Mack scrutinized the scene.

There was a genuine philosophical care in it but something specious too, not that Sam and Chris were false, nor Van and Trunk, but that Mack himself was suddenly cognizant of his artificiality and was not ready for this scene, as a character.

"Do I have to pay for your suggestion?" he wanted to know.

"Oooh, there is no pay for you. Just you will put us in your next completed novel, please."

"You do not pay," Chef Sam Orion tutted. "We have been waiting for you to come to us, so that we can let you know of your missing he."

"I don't understand," Mack almost cried.

"He is a subject." Chef Sam Orion. "In grammar."

"A subject does something." Chris Two-Side.

"Him is an object." Chef Sam.

"And an object has things done to it." Chris.

"You are missing your subject." Sam.

"You have become only object." Chris.

"You only let things happen to you." Sam.

"I am an object?" Mack tried.

"Yes!" they both shouted.

"Thank you."

"Find the he," said Chef Orion. "But hurry. We have our next customer."

Mack also knew that this little gap of respite was about to end.

Sure enough, the novelist crashed through the window, sprinting straight into it, spraying glass like water.

Van and Trunk attempted to react, but the novelist still had the power to grab their heads and shape them into one head and soon into one body.

He crammed them smaller and smaller in his hands into a ball, and the two minor characters became so compressed that they turned into a single bolus of a bullet.

The bullet of Van and Trunk was slid into the writer's empty gun and Mack saw it shot, saw it coming toward his left eye.

He moved and the bullet shot through the consecutive hearts of Chef Sam Orion and Chris Two-Side.

Mack ran.

This bullet ran after him.

The bullet re-grew in size.

It sprouted legs.

In fact it metamorphosed back into the novelist who could not keep up with Mack Harris.

What, then, was the writer's muscle?

He could murder some characters but not others.

He could become a bullet just to catch up with Mack, yet he couldn't quite catch him.

Just what was the writer's power?

Who, truthfully, was the writer?

As he wondered about this, he was certain he had seen Chloe behind him running with Sam, his psychiatrist (not poor dead Chef Sam Orion).

The he of the he-him.

Why was it missing?

The he-him.

Where was the he?

CHAPTER TWENTY-FOUR
The Subway

Even though he knew he had no power over himself if, in truth, he was more a character and less an author, he considered taking a train to Canada from Port Authority, maybe stopping to see his brother, Ford, along the way.

He longed for a quiet, hypnotic Amtrak to move him away from this chaos.

Inside himself, he was a city of mental traffic and truncated streets and vertical buildings.

He was no different than Manhattan, no different at all.

In front of him was the sneering novelist.

The moon was large and ridiculous, thick as moist pizza dough, and a stench rose up from garbage on the sidewalks and taxi cab exhaust.

Behind him now were Chloe and the psychiatrist.

He stood at the top of stairs to the 1 train, a red encircled 1 beckoning him.

He ran down the concrete steps.

Trains did not run frequently at this hour.

Soon it would be morning.

The novelist was not even running.

He used his MTA card and casually entered the turnstile.

Chloe and the psychiatrist did the same a few minutes later.

They were the only ones in the subway.

So it would be here.

It would all happen underground.

He doubted he would even make it a few stops up to Port Authority.

Forgetting his train to Toronto for the moment, he turned to look at the three people.

The fact that they were not in a hurry puzzled him.

He was treed like a rabbit now, nowhere to go.

The novelist walked right up to him.

Chloe and the psychiatrist chatted like intimates about fifty feet away.

Mack prayed for a train.

"Well, Mack," said the novelist, "can we stop the sprinting at least?"

"I guess."

"Look, you have to know some things before our gruesome last scene together occurs."

"Okay," said Mack, suspicious.

"There is someone higher than us."

"What do you mean?"

"I speak not of God, just someone higher. Our problems reside therein."

"How so?"

"I'm not a novelist, Mack, nor are you. You are a character. I am a character. We are both characters."

"You are a character?"

"I am," confessed the novelist. "I no more wrote this book than you did."

"Then why do I perceive that I am the author, that I am head sick, that I am fabricating you, that I'm not a character at all sometimes."

"You've evolved. I think you have found the he of the he-him finally. Intellectually, at least. You have yet to fully accept your inner character, though."

"What will happen here? I mean, shouldn't you have killed me back then at the restaurant? Didn't all the dramatic tension deflate after that?"

"This happens in literary novels, always some sort of subversive hatred of banal plots. Don't worry, the tension will resume in a bit. Chloe and the psychiatrist are lurking over there, and I can assure you that a bad thing is about to happen to me."

"To *you*? But you are supposed to be the novelist."

"I'm a temp, Mack. I was hired to distract you from the one who is higher than we are."

"You're a temp?"

"Yeah. They paid for my expenses and that apartment across the hall that you think I have. I was supposed to check in on you and keep you drunk as much as possible once they realized you were evolving so much. No character with a mental illness has ever prospered like you. But with that progress, you have attracted the attention of the one higher."

"Can't we be friends?" asked Mack.

"I wish we could. I like you a lot. We had good times."

"Aren't we the same person though?"

"Yeah, but that's irrelevant. We still had good times."

The novelist pulled out a copy of *Mack Harris Is Morbid*, as well as an expensive pen that wrote in dipped ink.

The nib was ornate as a shield.

"Please sign my copy. I don't think I'll ever have another chance for a character to sign an author's book, whoever that author happens to be."

"I'm not the author."

"You are, in a way."

As Mack held the novel, he motioned with his fingers to the "novelist" to hand him the pen, but it was in this moment of catastasis that his former friend aimed to blind him with the writing instrument.

The pen was so close to Mack's eye that ink dripped onto his pupil, burning his vision into a black blur.

Mack held the wrist off, and with his unblurry eye he noticed Chloe coming at him.

He couldn't believe that the novelist was a temp.

In the distance a slow 1 train finally approached, clicking on the tracks.

The psychiatrist hadn't noticed that Chloe was leaving him.

The tableau vivant was thus:

1) Mack Harris and the temp novelist struggling.
2) An expensive pen hovering over Mack's left eye.
3) Chloe, the eye model, seemed to want to help, pulling what looked like mace from her small purse.

4) A night train screamed in its approach.

5) The psychiatrist ran after her.

6) Mack struggled with the novelist, his left eye filling with ink. He would not be wounded by a temp.

7) As the train came, he found the strength to crack the wrist of his supposed drinking friend.

8) The pen fell into his free hand and in two quick thrusts, one in each eye, he blinded the pseudo-novelist as if the pen was sinking into the soft bruise on a baby's head.

9) And he watched the lethargic train knock the man's head back into a pole.

"Let Oscar go!" Chloe screamed.

"Oscar?" replied Mack, his own inked eye in excruciating blind pain. "Your ex?"

"I'm sorry, but he needed the job. I couldn't pay my rent. I'm sorry he came after you like this."

Mack blinked again and again to flush the ink from his eye.

Oscar, the novelist, the temp, the old drinking friend, whoever he was, lay bleeding from his eyes.

The train had merely bounced him right back onto the platform, wrenching his neck.

From under his eyelids seeped dark blood on the filthy concrete.

Chloe fell to the ground and covered Oscar's eyes futilely; the hands could not stop the blood.

The psychiatrist turned and ran, and Mack wished to leave this human warping in himself.

He was breathing so fast.

What just happened was disjointed, fragmented.

It defied climax.

Gradually, the ink flushed from his tormented eye.

A faster train approached, much faster than the last.

By their hair, Mack picked up Chloe and Oscar, one clump in each hand.

They seemed to welcome it, Oscar nearly dead anyway.

There was no conductor in front, an empty driver, no one to see Mack push the heads forward, their bodies yanked along like flotsam in a wave.

After the train passed, he saw no bodies on the tracks.

He could not stop gasping.

But he thought he was released from the inscrutable.

He welcomed the scrutable.

CHAPTER TWENTY-FIVE
Musical Interval

Breathing so heavy that he had to prop his hands on his thighs, Mack Harris tried to slow the gasps.

So he had murdered the novelist, finally, but there was nothing right about it because the guy supposedly wasn't a novelist at all, just a temporary worker.

The question was: could he believe what had happened?

If so, who *had* hired Oscar to be the novelist?

He had been chased for how many pages now, sometimes thinking he was just a homeless schizophrenic, sometimes believing he was the writer of *Mack Harris Is Morbid*, sometimes wondering if there was any novelist at all and sometimes assuming that he and the novelist were one person.

If the latter was the case, that his perception was disfigured and he was an insane writer who couldn't accept his illness, well, he could accept this.

And yet, his gut feeling, his truest intuition told him that more was happening.

For example, how could he be in the title *and* be the author?

It made no sense unless it was a memoir.

Jesus, not a memoir. Memoirs were awful. Puerile diaries.

And this was clearly a novel.

When Dumb Head had asked him to sign his first book, had Mack misread the cover?

Was he just so flattered that someone thought he was an author that he went along with the ego compliment?

Was he simply a misguided, puppeted character, albeit an evolved one?

He didn't buy it.

Had to be more to it.

Had to be.

As he breathed slower, he reached into one pocket and pulled out a fifty-dollar bill, staring at that drunk, Ulysses S. Grant.

He held it up to the light with two hands, not understanding how he had come to possess it.

Quick dog head shake from side to side.

Little man crunch was gone.

Van and Trunk.

Even the novelist.

He should be despondent.

He was not.

He was elated with this found money and a moment to spend it.

His impulse was to go to the first bar he saw and drink himself into the morning.

And so six hours passed, beer after beer.

It was noon or something like noon.

Six more hours passed.

It was six p.m., maybe.

Six more hours.

Midnight.

He found himself drunk on a 6 train holding onto a metal pole, bullied by the mannequin bodies around him.

The doors blasted open at Spring St. with a sssss and he climbed some stairs and was lost when he stood at the corner of several streets intersecting.

Since he could never remember exact details, he had to triangulate former memories to come back to places he had once been.

After a superfluity of wrong lefts and rights, he found the sign. He saw the door.

He walked down the steps into the dark place.

To the lovely redhead with sad eyes, he said: "Do you still have room for me?"

She nodded and took his fifty, giving him back a twenty.

"You get two free drinks with that," she informed him.

Mack parted the purple velvet curtain.

On a small stage just ten feet away from him was a young blond goateed man in black-rimmed glasses playing a trombone with an organist, sax and drummer.

A middle-aged couple, a white woman and a black man, drank from martini glasses at their table.

Mack was ushered to his seat and he watched and listened as the jazz came.

Come on jazz, come to me.

He thought of the seclusion of churches, the fussiness of relationships, the endless reverberations of death, but they were supplanted by the plaintive, real sound coming from the trombonist who was snapping his fingers to begin a new song.

Into the mike he spoke, "This next song is called 'The Cobbler' and I wrote it when I was jonesin' to eat some cobbler after a gig."

The trombonist visored his eyes with his hand to keep from being blinded by the spotlight.

"And is that my man Mack Harris out in the audience I see?"

How did he know him?

"Thanks for comin', Mack. Sendin' you over some free beers. One of our best fans. Always finds us when we play. A-one, a-two ..."

The music kicked and oh it kicked with both legs.

The organ and trombone blended into almost sapid notes of honey and butter that you could taste.

Next, the sax soloed as the trombonist nodded in appreciation. Drum solo, organ solo, back to trombone.

Mack's life, if a life could be music, was jazz.

It was jazz because there was form with an inversion of form.

It was jazz because it was an expected sound with unexpected moments.

He could not feel this in church.

And he guessed he had seen these musicians before because the bandleader knew him.

He couldn't remember when he had seen them last.

He hated that he had no memory of the good in him.

Then again, he loved that he never repeated an experience and came to things he had already done with virgin eyes.

Maybe he had seen jazz two-hundred times.

Maybe thirty.

He recalled none of those times, at least in his head.

His body remembered.

Instinct brought him back to this club, even if the specifics were blurred.

Hadn't he wandered the streets with no direction only to end up exactly where he had wanted to be?

His hands had not stopped trembling from the murder of the novelist.

A free beer was sent over by the bandleader.

Mack gulped it down his throat and another was placed in front of him.

Alcohol and jazz encircled his head like two planets in an orbit.

Maybe jazz was the sun, beer the moon.

It was said that the trombone was the closest instrument to the human voice, and why the trombonist always sat in the center of an orchestra.

Mack listened and could hear sweet voices in the trombone lulling him away from dreadful thoughts.

What time had he gotten here?

Midnight?

He gulped down another beer.

What time was it?

Two a.m.?

Another set, more beer.

What time?

Six a.m.?

Had the quartet played all night?

How many sets?

There were never enough sets.

Why was live jazz only played at night, never the day?

Jazz was the night sun.

It couldn't be the moon.

Stumbling from his seat, he felt a hand on his shoulder.

The trombonist. "You okay, Mack?"

"I'm okay, I'm okay."

"Thanks for comin' to the gig. Kept us goin'."

"What time is it?"

"Man, it's six a.m.! We played the whole night."

So Mack had the time right for once in his life.

They shook hands.

Mack didn't want to leave.

He hoped he would see jazz and this musician again.

He remembered goodness.

The musician was good, a good man.

Maybe jazz *felt* like the sun, even if it was played in the dark. Yes, that was it.

Up the stairs he struggled, his body lethargic, his mind bright with inner radiance.

The morning sun blinded him.

He visored his eyes like the trombone player had under the spotlight.

And for the next six hours, he walked.

He stopped in a bar that was actually open and drank.

He missed the novelist.

Some part of him was missing.

All the details didn't yield any kind of clarification.

After leaving the bar, he stumbled into the rain and found a newspaper to cover his head.

As he moved through the city with no purpose, he wondered who he really was, if he was anyone at all.

Externality had preoccupied him for a long time.

Too long.

Jazz, rain, murders.

Good or bad, they were distractions from the internal, the sacred.

It was an issue of identity, never knowing exactly who you were, never receiving the right clues, always feeling self-baffled.

The he-him.

CHAPTER TWENTY-SIX
A Familiar Film

The saturated newspaper covering his wet hair was useless in the rain.

He also had the hiccups and felt comically human, doused by a wetness coating him like paint, a different paint from the blood that once dripped down his eyes in that church, a better simile than blood.

Finally, he tossed the soggy paper in a city trash can that was too full of paper cups and walked up to the ticket window.

"Hic, one please," he said, shivering.

"Skksaa."

"I'm sorry?" he spoke into the window at the girl with black spiked hair.

"Thank you," she must have said into her microphone, which Mack heard again as "skksaa".

There was only a single film showing and he hadn't even checked the marquee for its title.

He pocketed his ticket and rushed inside, thinking about the overview effect of astronauts when they see Earth from another place, the euphoria they feel.

His hunger often gave him the same feeling.

As he entered the lobby, he did a capriole causing the popcorn vendor to eye his mischievous skip.

Hic.

"'The Lord is my light,'" Mack said under his breath. "Psalm twenty-seven."

As he thought of twenty-seven, he was insistent that it be perceived as twenty-seven (and not 27).

No numbers right now.

Numbers = *numb*ers.

Rhyming was a child.

Poetry was an adult.

Some poets needed to play, rhyme more.

More caprioles please.

He came to the young man with crossed eyes in a wheelchair, tearing tickets.

His body was in a ball and he had no legs.

On his bald head were two foot-long blond strands that resembled flaccid corn silk.

They were in thin braids.

"Theater's just behind you," he rasped, handing Mack one half of the ticket.

"Thank, hic, you."

Mack just stood there.

"Wait, you're Mack Harris."

"Yes, why?"

"You're a mystagogue."

"I'm sorry, what?"

"Your visions, I mean, your book, you know. I believe in your visions. I apologize for bothering you."

"Hm," Mack mumbled.

"Your book saved me, my life."

"It did?"

"Yes."

"Thank you for saying it, hic."

"Um, enjoy your movie."

Inside the theater of about fifty seats, Mack was the only person.

He sat in the very front row.

The screen was not a big one.

Good.

He liked small screens.

And while he didn't know exactly what he was about to see, he was certain it would be noirish.

Somehow, he usually found the movie he wanted, even when he didn't plan on it.

People recognized him.

They knew his face.

Mystagogue, hic?

On the floor at his feet was a piece of popcorn that caught his attention.

Since the screen was blank, he needed to cerebrate on something.

Impulsively, still with the hiccups, he began to notice errant popcorn everywhere.

He stood.

It was dotted up and down the carpet like floor stars.

He walked the aisle, back and forth, counting each piece, awed by the sudden prolificity he had missed upon entering.

He moved side to side behind the seats, in front of the seats.

Refusing to touch the filthy junk food, he nevertheless mentally counted the specks as the insipid previews flashed on the screen.

He ignored them but was aware that they had begun.

He *had* to count all the popcorn on the floor, moving like a vagile fish darting around in an aquarium.

Soon, he would be more like coral, his sessility rendering him immobile as he sat and drooled at the screen.

He was running throughout the theater and sweating and hiccupping when his ursine frame eventually fell into his seat, sweat dripping down his forehead like icicles on a warm day.

The credits of the film began.

Mack watched.

His hiccups stopped.

His eyes blurred with sweat and he missed being able to read what was on the screen.

After rubbing his eyes, he saw four words he recognized.

A frisson was electric in his head and body.

He thought of that word's origins tied to *friction* from the French *friçon* but also connected to *frigid.*

It was a perfect moment for etymological derivation because he felt a cold friction in him.

The white words on the black screen read: MACK HARRIS IS MORBID.

Mack looked around the theater to see if he was still alone.

He was.

More credits.

BASED ON THE NOVEL BY MARK DAMON PUCKETT.

Mack jumped to his feet.

But wait, he thought.

Didn't I kill the novelist?

Or didn't I figure out that I was inventing the novelist, that he was never real, and that when I killed him, I was in fact merging his death into me?

Didn't I think I was the writer at one point???

And finally: who the hell is Mark Damon Puckett?!

"You're not the writer," a voice shouted from the back.

"Who's that? Quiet, the movie's starting."

A shadow walked toward him, emerging as a young man with the eyes of a hawk.

He sat beside Mack and the hair on their forearms rubbed.

"Hi, I'm Mark. Mark Damon Puckett."

Meanwhile, the movie had started.

Oddly enough, the same scene happening in the theater was occurring on the screen, synchronous, so that the two characters would not miss anything and be able to clear up some novelistic matters.

"Wait," Mack said, dumbfounded. "That's the exact scene that's happening right here."

"Yes," said Mark. "We planned it that way."

"I'm so lost, man."

"That's my fault," Mark assured him. "I'm here to explain, then I hope we can watch the film. Once we are done talking, the movie will stop mimicking this scene, although the scene is important."

"I can't keep up anymore, Mark."

"I know. I know. Mack, it's okay. But it's also simple. First, *Mack Harris Is Morbid* is a book, a novel, my novel. You are the protagonist in that book."

"But what about all these people who think it's mine, that I'm the actual author? Dumb Head, the coffee guy? Even the ticket ripper outside?"

"It was hard to keep you guessing. So curious."

"And the novelist I killed? He turned out to simply be some kind of delusion of myself? The way I see it is that I wrote the book, that the novelist who was my supposed neighbor was not real, that he was really myself, and that I came to understand my schizophrenia through writing this second book, *The Killer Detective Novelist*, and I am *not* an actual character. Why else would people recognize me on the streets, if I wasn't the author?"

"All good points, Mack. You finished?"

"I am, I guess. I *saw* the book though. Dumb Head showed it to me. It said my name, Mack Harris, and I signed it in pencil."

"Look, you often perceive beautiful things, but you also misperceive and cannot be trusted. That's why I created you. Your fallibility makes you an empyrean of literary characters. You saw your name in the title and thought you were the author. That's all."

Mark pulled out a copy of the first novel from his shoulder bag. *Mack Harris Is Morbid* by Mark Damon Puckett. He handed it to Mack.

"I don't believe it."

"It's a signed copy," said Mark.

"What! I don't want a signed copy from you. Authors aren't supposed to give their characters signed copies."

"Take it, so we can watch the movie."

In this moment Mack had a salient awareness he was not real.

He clutched the novel in his hands and held it in front of him.

The film continued to mimic this gesture.

The Greek for mind was *noos*; he was asphyxiating on the end of an imaginative rope.

On the other hand, how often did characters get to hang out with their creators?

"We just can't do this in the third novel, okay?" Mark whispered. "Now that you're so aware."

"Understandable."

"I'm not supposed to be here, but I've been feeling very guilty for your confusion. You probably feel some sort of ongoing fustigative pain from the plot pummeling I've run you through."

"Yeah, I'm not a lab rat, Mark."

"Of course. You've done well through two books. And that novelist, or faux novelist, across the hall was never real. He was meant to be a part of you that made you wonder if you yourself were writing the books. That's all. You figured it out over time. And there are two books, not one. You were right all along."

Mack sighed and looked at Mark Damon Puckett.

On his head was a peruke, one of those absurd white wigs from the 17th century.

How had he missed it?

Maybe he was too focused on the intrusion into his theater, his sanctuary.

Maybe he had too much adrenalin and ire in him to think straight, once he learned about who he was, or in this case, who he was not.

He was not an author.

The author was right here.

He was a strong character, a character that was also in a film.

But his character was strong.

At this point, the movie altered itself from mimicking them, and the filmic Mack Harris, who was played by an actor resembling him exactly, began to speak to the filmic little man crunch, who was obviously not in the cinema.

"Crunch!"

The little man crunch!

He missed crunch.

"Crunch," Mark repeated, with a sigh.

"Ah yes, crunch," Mack said, grinning.

"Oh," said the actual novelist, "I have something else for you."

Mack turned to him. "What's that?"

Mark pulled another book out of his bag.

The Killer Detective Novelist.

"W-wait," Mack stuttered, "but how did you write the last part of this if we are still here? Now that's just impossible."

Mark stared at him with expectation.

Mack, at last, nodded in further awareness.

"You already knew the ending," Mack said, seeing it all.

"Yes, I did."

"Because you're the writer."

"That's right."

"And I pretty much don't exist."

"Yes, I'm very sorry, Mack."

Without speaking, Mack Harris, the fictional character, watched Mack Harris in the movie, while sitting beside the actual novelist who had written the book.

It was a decent version of *Mack Harris Is Morbid*, albeit not nearly cerebral enough for Mack and Mark's tastes.

Film was too passive, never coming close to the involvedness of novels anyway.

As he stared at the screen, Mack realized that he had two signed copies from the author as proof that he was merely a character, should he ever need them in the future.

In many ways, Mack was relieved he wasn't a writer while simultaneously dreading himself as a character in the ensuing third novel.

Was it possible for a character to kill his author?

Mark turned to him without speaking. *I know what you're thinking, Mack.*

Mack stared at Mark; they could not exist without each other.

They both stared back at the film.

Perhaps it was better to be nescient in the end, they both thought at the exact same time, for when you didn't know anything, you never asked questions.

ISBN: 9780983543503
Author: Mark Damon Puckett
Publisher: Onion Scribe Publishing
Learn more at:
www.markdamonpuckett.com

"*The Reclusives* by Mark Damon Puckett had me laughing out loud, in public places. Every story is unique insight into the beauty of our internal thoughts as individuals living in a very externally driven world. The stories acknowledge a shallowness that exists in people and our way of living everyday conversation . . . but the way they acknowledge it, is by great depth. Provocative, puzzling, and bizarre, but always honest and vivid. It moves like we move."

—CRITIC ERIN BOYLAN

". . . . a very worthwhile experience, especially for those drawn to the accessibly avant-garde."

—CLAYTON LACHMUND,
author of *The Innocence*

"With *The Reclusives*, Mark Puckett has written a gem of a collection. Each story is what a writer might scrawl on the backs of rejection letters for submissions that followed the rules set by workshops and literary journals. The language is impatient and emphatic, stating directly those first associations of image and meaning that come from the creation of narrative made of the observed absurdity of daily life. Freer and more open to asymmetric logic than the typical short story, each reflects the psychology of their protagonists, who, while recluses, are not rejects. Rather Puckett's characters are recluses from the hypocrisy of the cliches that construct the go-nowhere 9-to-5 work-a-day world. Their inability to remain tidily numbed by the sedative of no-meaning makes them unable to just be. A salary man discovers the cubicles of his office have the internal logic of a multi-floor crossword puzzle. A novelist finds success only by writing unpublishable novels in the voice of a Czech literary figure who does not exist. A Willy Lomanesque businessman has his moment of self discovery in the halls of a dog show among artificially coiffed poodles. And in the extended final piece, 'Pool Man', Puckett lets rip an ecstatic freebase of an odyssey with twist after twist through an absurdist but eminently logical landscape that folds one moment upon the next. All the while, Puckett manages to maintain a sweet regard for his 'reclusives', allowing each character the opportunity within their story to achieve a certain uneasy peace with themselves, their positions in this whacked out world, and move on into whatever awaits them beyond. The results are frequently curious, never quite what is expected and always very smart. I can heartily recommend his work to those for whom the status quo feels a bit more like a strait-jacket. This is a good book and one worth taking for a swim."

—POET JORN AKE,
author of *Asleep in the Lightning Fields*,
The Circle Line and *Boys Whistling Like Canaries*

"In these nine stories Mark Damon Puckett doesn't just run the gamut, he runs laps, caroming from character to character and a variety of experiences, with each tale leaving an indelible mark. A wonderful collection."

—NOVELIST JEFF GOMEZ,
author of *Our Noise, Geniuses of Crack*
and *Attempted Chemistry*

"Impeccable. This is simply a great read! Too often, short stories are so driven by theme that they fail to pull the reader in through the characters. As a writer of novels and a reader who likes to be pushed and pulled on an emotional level as well as an intellectual one, I found Mark Damon Puckett's collection a pleasure. The writing is exceptional, but where *The Reclusives* truly shines is within its quirky and haphazard assortment of human beings. This book will make you think and feel and laugh out loud as you see myriad parts of yourself, and everyone you've ever met, come to life. These are stories that will stay with you long after the book has been read."

—NOVELIST WENDY WALKER,
author of *Four Wives* and *Social Lives*

"Just tore through *The Reclusives*, simply because it is one of the easiest tomes I've read in a long time! The characters are so compelling, so accurate—I *know* these people, man! These are real people. Reclusive? Yes. Neurotic, you bet. A cross-section of the underworld ethos of a misanthropic, neophytic, awkwardly social generation. And I raise my glass to them and celebrate each of them! For without *them*, who are *we*?! I truly enjoyed it. I laughed out loud, and I empathized. Great characters, and wonderfully delicate stories."

—TODD DUFFEY,
Actor, *Office Space* and *Buffy the Vampire Slayer*

"Puckett's characters invite themselves into your consciousness and then start rearranging the furniture. You're never quite sure who let them in, but once inside, they're there to stay. They're odd, damaged creatures, these people—somehow both ingratiating and rude at the same time—in other words, strange as they are, they're real."

—DAVID THOMPSON,
London Critic

YOU with The Ill-usives

ISBN: 9780983543510
Author: Mark Damon Puckett
Publisher: Onion Scribe Publishing
Learn more at:
www.markdamonpuckett.com